All or Nothing

A Charlie Ford Adventure

Book Three

By Mike Evans

To all my fans and supporters, thank you for still loving to read this near and dear to my heart.

****

This Book is licensed for your personal enjoyment upon purchase. Thanks for respecting this author's work.

Thank you for reading! I do hope that you enjoy it!

Edited by Elizabeth Robbins Editing Services

I would like to thank my special team of beta readers, these folks are amazing, Leslie and Karen.

You can find all things Mike Evans related at

MIKE EVANS AUTHOR WEBSITE
https://www.mikeevansauthor.com/

Mike's newsletter don't miss out on any news! I will NOT SPAM YOU.
http://www.tinyurl.com/evansnews

Mike Evans Facebook Author Page
https://www.facebook.com/MikeEvansAuthor

Contact Email
m.evansauthor@gmail.com

Mike Evans on Amazon
https://www.amazon.com/Mike-Evans/e/B00IQ9Z75A

Stand-alone and Series by Mike Evans

Charlie Ford Adventure Series
The Orphans Series
Gabriel Series
The Uninvited Series
Demons Beware Series
Zombies and Chainsaws
Zombies on The Block Series
Deal with The Devil
Buried: Broken oaths
Voices in My Head
The Operator

Prologue

Jim and Tim had moved aboard onto the boat. The three of them, Charlie, Jim, and Tim had been busy fielding phone calls. It made Charlie a firm believer in the fact that any promotion or any publicity is good publicity. He quite frankly could have murdered Jim at the time when he had spouted off that they were going to be opening up shop in the Keys.

It was made worse by a simple fact that he hadn't asked the two of them beforehand. None of them currently had a job nor had they any plans. Jim and Tim didn't have much of an excuse but had both seriously enjoyed their time of freedom, free from being told what to do, where to eat, when to eat, etc.

The best thing about his two best friends in the world besides, they were both amusing as hell was that if you needed something done then they were the ones to make that happen and always have your back. Jim had been bitching for an entire month, but Tim and Charlie had told him to go to hell. There would be nothing started until his dumbass was up, able, and available to help. Investigating was something that the two of them had been doing for the last decade or so. But this venture was going to be a partnership, not a one man shop where one guy did all the work and the other two got to take it easy and collect the checks.

Charlie had felt guilty about Jim getting shot, but that had worn thin pretty quick after having to be his wet nurse for a month. But in Charlie's defense, it had not been his intention to have that happen to his buddy. Charlie later on had reflected on the fact that he had purposely driven the lawyer Mr. Twain's car head on directly towards Bruno and Lou and the other two. Charlie had realized when all was said and done that it probably would have been the exact same reaction that he would have had if somebody was purposely choosing to T-bone him. But unfortunately, they'd had time to shoot, and Jim had caught a bullet to the arm.

By the time they were getting done with things as far as cleaning up the boat and adding a few amenities so three grown men could all live aboard, it had taken a decent amount of time, but it wasn't too bad. Anytime Jim had complained how long it was taking, they would happily mention if he wasn't currently a one-armed man then things might go a little quicker. It typically was enough to shut him up, which quite frankly made everybody pretty happy.

Chapter 1

La Familia

"Marcos, did you get the information that we needed? I would like to know exactly what went wrong the other night."

"Sir?"

"I've sunk at least a half million into the idea of him taking the Keys over. I can get the perfect spot if I have him in charge. I could never do anything here if his old man was in charge."

Marcos thought about what he was going to say. He knew that there was a slim line between saying the right thing, and having your feet cut off and tossed out in the middle of the desert. He said, "There weren't too many people to get details from, Sr. Juan Jose."

"Marcos, are you trying to piss me off? Did I ask you for an excuse or an answer?"

"No sir, quite literally I had to wait for one of our guys who were keeping track of them to check on things and get back to me. I tried calling every single person in Junior's bar and didn't have any answers. We drove through trying to check on our or I mean your investment, sir, and it had been shot to shit. I'm not talking drive by; I'm talking someone pulled up with the US Army but only had them fire on one space with no stopping. I was surprised it didn't implode from the roof's weight."

"He's such an idiot. You could have gotten anyone; you thought the best idea was putting father against son?"

"Sir, the situation had a few ways to play out. What happened, what we wanted to happen, and above all else, the most ideal situation is that they all killed each other and then we just swooped in to take over everything else."

"That didn't happen, now did it?"

"No, it didn't, but I'm going to make it right. I wouldn't let you down again. I promise you."

"Marcos?"

"What sir?"

"I meant you couldn't let me down more than two times because that is when I will murder you with my own two bare hands."

"I probably should have started off with saying the good news first."

"Wow, whose nephew are you? Are you someone's nephew or son or did you marry in? There's no way you made it this long being that stupid without someone having a reason to not murder you. If you are unsure than let me make this as clear for you as fucking possible. You need to always start with the good news. Do you know how close I was to killing you?"

"I'd like to think not too close, but I don't believe that to be true, now is it?"

"No, I was thinking I'd be happy to murder you. What is the good news?"

"Nydegger, he was the one who was arranging things for his kid. He's a lawyer, you know the type that everyone goes to when they need some shady shit written up, so it doesn't look quite so shady?"

"Fucking hate lawyers."

Marcos asked, "Did you want to talk to the lawyer, by chance? There was no question about it though the number of people still alive after all that was said and done is not a large number."

"Bring him to me the minute you lay eyes on him."

Chapter 2

One month after the night of shooting

Charlie had gone down the list of potential clients and looked at what the details were for each person. He had it set up so that when they were ready to start working that they could simply pick all the easiest shit first, preferably stuff that would hopefully not get them shot, which was definitely on top of Jim's list. But they had been having a few issues with getting their private investigator licenses with special permits to carry in the Keys.

They wanted to do everything on the up and up, and even though Jim had mentioned how many of the things they had on their list that didn't need to necessarily be with finger quotes as he said "reported" finger quotes Charlie had explained with no question that absolutely was not going to be the way. He and Tim both wanted to do everything right. They knew that in almost all occupations that having a good reputation meant everything.

Charlie wasn't necessarily one to call in favors. He'd tried to get the license correctly and without pulling favors. But after the third time in a month of rejection letters coming he'd researched how you actually get the papers. He wasn't shocked but was definitely annoyed when he realized that the local police department needed to give a sign of the cross and blessing before you were able to get one. So, he'd not needed to put too much thought into the fact that one of the large reasons why he might not be getting the license for the three of them could have been Detective Lindvall throwing a few wrenches in their way.

Charlie had seriously hoped that the proof he had tucked away would have been plenty to put him off of wanting to screw with the three of them. But alas that had not ended up being the case, which definitely pissed Charlie off a bit. The loss of money from Junior dying might have been part of everything.

Charlie was reading the letter aloud saying, "Another fucking denial, damn it!"

Jim said, "Are you using crayon to fill them out, Charlie?"

"Oh, you are just fantastic. Tim, I see you smiling. Do not entice him to continue his reign of stupid questions. No, you wouldn't know this because I've done it all three times."

"You act like that's a big deal. This is your third denial. I mean, what does it matter if you keep getting denied?"

"I wouldn't usually hit a cripple, but damn, I am really, really considering it, Jim."

"So, since you have a giant heart and aren't going to hit me, what are we going to do about the license, Mr. Ford? I mean, if you're so adamant about having one and we can't get one, then when the hell do we actually get to open up shop?"

"First, you need to be less gimpy. And I'm not talking about your fully healed gimpy. I'm talking about your one bad arm that needs to be healed gimpy; we can handle two arm gimpy Jim…"

Jim cut him off, "I'm sorry. How many times do you think you can say gimpy in a sentence?"

Charlie answered saying, "Well, gimpy, I can't even say how many times I could possibly say gimpy to a gimpy gimpy guy like you. I mean, it would almost be impossible to count the number of gimps that I can spout off. But since you're so kind to ask what I'm going to do, or sorry, *we* are going to do, which actually means me even though you're the one that can't do any real labor at the moment, I guess as little as I like doing it, I might need to call in a favor."

"With who? I mean, me and Tim are basically the only two people you know down here."

Tim asked, "You realize we're banking an entire idea for a living off of something he said while delirious from getting shot and having a pretty decent amount of blood loss right?"

Jim said, "Whoa, whoa, whoa, whoa, it doesn't matter if I was a little delirious or not, a good idea is a good idea. So, like I said to Charlie, what are you going to do about getting us a license?"

Charlie said, "If you'd stop bickering then I could just tell you that I'm going to call Mr. Fratto. I'm hoping to see if he knows anyone that might be able to push our license through a little bit faster."

"Sorry, I know I'm the slow one of the group. But we're going to go to the mob so that way we can get a legitimate legal license, right?"

Tim slapped Jim on the good arm, still making him wince, saying, "See and everyone calls him the stupid one. I mean he is, but he can figure out basic things like two plus two, mob bosses with connections. He's not as dumb as everyone says...all the time."

Charlie replied, "Well if there's anything that's a better idea please tell me now. Because, if this makes us even, great. But if it makes it so that we owe him something then that might not be so awesome."

"Charlie, Tim, what's the big deal if we owe an organized mob boss a favor? You act like we've never had that issue before."

Charlie was nodding, saying, "Well it could be because we have never had that before. I really do think maybe you ate too many paint chips as a kid, Jim."

"I don't know why everyone assumes that I ate paint chips. I mean have you ever smelled gas? It's intoxicating."

Charlie held back a shit-eating grin as he hopped off the boat saying, "Tim, make sure that Jim gets his nap. Make sure you change him too. We don't want to worry about that rash coming back. I'll be back in a couple hours; I'm going to get a few things done after I see Fratto."

Tim said, "Can I give him his painkiller, now? It really would be nice if he took a nap."

"But I'm not even tired," Jim said.

"Actually, screw him. Charlie, how about I leave Jim up on deck and I can go take a nap? I can't really say that I give a shit if he sleeps, and to be honest, you won't be here so he's not going to annoy anyone."

Charlie said, "I think I'm just going to let the two of you work this out. Best of luck though, Tim. I'm sure everything's gonna go great."

Chapter 3

Nydegger Law Offices Esquire

Lisa was sitting at her secretary's desk. She'd felt no warm safe feelings when she'd come in and opened up the office. Lisa had already been terrified when she saw the building and the current state of it a month ago. Nydegger had gotten everything fixed but the memory of everything was still strong. Lisa realized today might not be great when two men she didn't know walked in. They didn't seem like they cared whatsoever that she was there as a witness, someone who could call the police, basically she might as well have not been there at all.

Lisa tried to smile without looking like she was going to be sick at the exact same time. There were a lot of names running through her head at the moment. Names like CareerBuilder, Zip recruiter, LinkedIn, maybe anything, she didn't care. But she was sick of the idea that she didn't know on a daily basis sometimes that she would or would not live. It could be McDonald's, she thought, if it meant that Nydegger Esquire wasn't the first thing on the paper header.

She cleared her throat and said, "Good morning, gentlemen. Welcome to Nydegger Esquire Law Offices. What brought you in this morning? Did you have an appointment?"

The two men looked at each other, their knowing smiles filled her with enough confidence to make her want to put out an alert for herself in advance. The man whispered something to the other in Spanish. She wasn't very good at the language but needed to know a little living down in the Keys. She knew the basics and a few great phrases for when she'd had too many. But she was pretty sure that she'd just heard the word bitch and murder. Lisa was already trying to think if outrunning these two was in the least bit possible.

Lisa knew all the Pilates classes in the world wouldn't do shit if she needed to run. Lisa came to a quick conclusion, realizing going out for drinks with her friends had been a bigger part of her getting ready this morning than the possibility that she might be on her feet all day. Lisa had worn her high heels knowing that the extra inch put a little extra something into her stride when she went up to the bar. She wasn't necessarily looking for a man, but by God, if the right one crossed paths with her, she definitely would not give him a blind eye.

Lisa knew the first time she tried to run in the heels that laced up her ankle that she would snap her ankle bone through the skin with very little doubt. The race would be quick, pointless, and probably leave her on the ground begging for her life and crying. Lisa was starting to wonder why only convenience stores and bars seemed to have shotguns underneath the counter. She wasn't stupid, Lisa thought to herself. She knew how to pull the trigger or squeeze one or whatever you did with the little trigger thingy as good as anyone. She could be all badass like in Desperado and have a double barrel pistol shotgun. Of course, the recoil would probably snap her wrist when she shot it.

A loud clap brought her out of the daydream. She kind of looked around, remembering that there had been these two gentlemen which had set off her sense of needing to get out of there. Then recollected that she'd asked him a question. The two men appeared to be as opposite as they could between one in a black suit, the other a white, one bald and one had long oiled black hair. The I am going to die feeling that you got after almost getting into a car crash and dying was a feeling that she really was experiencing at the moment. Shiny head guy leaned on her desk and with a thick accent smiled. It looked like every other one of his teeth was gold not making

Lisa feel much better. She apologized, asking, "I'm sorry, my ears temporarily weren't working. I am really sorry, but would you mind repeating yourself for me?"

Shiny head man said, "You asked if we had an appointment. I had replied that we are looking for Nydegger Esquire. Is he in the office today?"

Lisa knew when dealing with clients it was always best to lie or at least when dealing with his clients it was best. Lisa also knew that until she knew what was going on it might not do her any good mentioning that he was here. She shrugged noncommittally saying, "If you like, I could maybe give him a call? I could see if he's in the office."

Shiny head man sat down on her desk saying calmly but with no positivity in his voice, "My name is Bernardo, and this is my cousin Luis. We are here to see Mr. Nydegger Esquire immediately. He isn't at home, and his car is out front, parked next to your red Toyota Camry, Lisa. We know that you've been here for about twenty minutes and that's because it takes you fifteen to get here from your lovely blue house…"

"I'm sorry, how do you know what I drive, or what color

my…"

"Please, a beautiful lady like you should not interrupt. It is rude, and you must have manners, right? I was just going to say your lovely blue house is at 6225 Hammock Drive in the Keys. Now please know you are muy bonita, and you could probably keep this dumb act up all day, but we are only here to see Nydegger…"

The other man had a lovely suit on but definitely did not seem at home in it. When he leaned up, his jacket fell to the wayside and showed something chrome under his coat. Lisa was pretty sure he didn't have it there to do anything good with. She remembered the good old days when Nydegger just dealt with crooked businessmen and women. No one showed up with guns, there wasn't much work that needed to be done in courtrooms, and there was nothing more invigorating than watching someone get a new lease on life, especially if they had a cheating husband or wife.

Lisa didn't know what she should do. The fact that they had guns and seemed to know some pretty intimate details about her like an unlisted address should not be available for people to know made matters feel even worse. Lisa held up her hands saying, "I'm going to ring back to his office. I need to use my hands to do this."

Greasy long-haired man said, "Yes, we know how to use a telephone."

Lisa did as she said she would and waited for the phone to be picked up, feeling like her life depended on it. She didn't want to betray Nydegger's confidence in her but thought there was a strong probability that the son of a bitch had run the first moment he saw these two standing in the entryway. When Lisa looked out the window, she needed to do a double take. Lisa thought that she was having a stroke. Everything she saw instantly had a red tint on it; she was pretty sure that it was Nydegger's yet to be spilt blood.

He wasn't an athlete, not even in the golf type. But she could see a not very well put together Nydegger hobbling across the blacktop. The look of anger and resentment in her eyes apparently had given away her poker hand. Both men looked over, seeing Nydegger racing the best that a scrawny lawyer could towards his car. If he'd still had a driver then Cliff probably would have still been there, and he could have let him know to just swoop over by the side entrance and they could get on out of there.

Greasy hair guy, who did seem to have all the anger in the world, took off. He didn't say anything. It would seem the job that they had to do was black and white, just like their suits. Lisa screamed when the man took off racing out the doors. His large figure did nothing to slow him down any and if she'd ever seen a lion going after its prey then this sure as shit was the human equivalent.

Nydegger tried to slow down, putting his hands up, realizing he wasn't going to get away. He tried to focus on the man as well as trying not to make obvious eye contact with Lisa who he could feel burning holes into his face. He'd never admit that they made eye contact but the look of hate along with a middle finger left no doubt about exactly how she felt right now.

Nydegger was waiting for the man to stop at any moment, any second really. Nydegger cringed a little when he figured out this man wasn't going to stop until his dumb ass had already taken flight. Shiny hair guy body checked the shit out of Nydegger, sending him backwards at least four feet in the air before he came to a grinding halt on the less than friendly pavement below, his head being quickly rubbed raw.

Nydegger left a blood splatter line of hair and skin. Nydegger tried to get up, but the man put a foot down on his chest. He could only assume who these guys were with. He had to think that possibly this was going to end up in a job offer but more than likely they would have approached this a little differently had that been the issue unless the job wasn't optional. Nydegger tried to sit up saying, "Sorry buddy, but I don't know if I'm accepting new clients right now."

The man still had his foot on his chest and pushed the heel of his steel-toed boots down until he could feel his heel moving across the bone. He started rotating it slowly back and forth making sure that he knew that with no question at all that he truly wanted this to hurt. Greasy hair guy bent down and dead-lifted Nydegger up off the ground holding him up while he got his footing beneath him. Once he did, the guy shoved Nydegger in front of him.

Nydegger walked in front of the man. His hands were out to the side, and he was limping a little bit, not necessarily loving the throbbing feeling in his chest. When he got into the building Nydegger said, "Lisa, are you okay?"

Lisa looked at him and didn't have to put much thought into what she wanted to say. She'd been thinking about saying, "Go fuck yourself, you god damn coward. You seriously fucking ran out the back door when I was trying to help you stay safe! Yeah, go to hell! I quit! I'm going to find out where Cliff's working. Maybe I can find a safer job where I could test drugs or maybe bullet proof vests. There's nothing in this world that would be worse than working for you. I'll test rectal thermometers up my ass if it means I never need to see your rat face again!"

Bald headed man put up a finger saying, "I'm only detaining you temporarily, but we need to have a conversation with your boss."

"Who's stopping you? I'll just head out and you won't have to see or deal with…"

He walked forward and when she held up her hands took one of her slim wrists making it look like a piece of licorice compared to himself and handcuffed her to the desk drawer. Lisa was fighting during this entire time. He said, "You need to stop doing this now, or I'm going to have to help you stop. I have no issues hitting a woman. It is probably part of that equality that no one wants to have rolled over with all those rights you probably want."

She was going to ask how long it would take or when she could leave. In the back of her mind, Lisa thought she could just call the police and then maybe they could come and let her go. If they got into a fire fight, maybe an added bonus would be that she could watch Nydegger get shot. She was thinking immediately that when they were out of sight that she would be googling very quickly how to remove a pair of handcuffs or at least the one which was attached to her wrist. The desk could keep its new fashion piece because she didn't ever plan on seeing it again. That idea went out the window when he reached over, lifting her monitor up and throwing it twenty feet away followed by her landline and motioned for her cell. She said, "Could you please not destroy that? I have a really long time left on that one."

He smiled, walking a few feet before placing it on a table in the sitting room. Lisa stopped struggling and watched as the three men walked down the hallway to the conference room or Nydegger's office, it was yet to be seen. She was very curious if the two of them would ever be seen again. If not, she couldn't really pretend that he'd be missed all that much. But she definitely wanted to try and not die today. She was way too young for that to happen.

Chapter 4

Charlie drove the only vehicle currently that the three of them had. Jim and Tim had a road trip down to the Keys and knew that whatever situation they were going to have to deal with in the Keys that there was a strong probability that it wasn't going to be pleasant all the time. One thing the three of them had learned quickly was that insurance payouts on trucks that were firebombed and exploded were not at the top of their list. However, it was not completely ideal having to share a truck regardless of how nice it was. The fact that for the first few weeks that Jim hadn't been allowed to drive with his arm in a sling and other than a few appointments at Dr. Kenny's, he'd not had a lot of reasons to leave the boat. Jim had taken doing nothing to all new levels. After they had originally gotten home from the hospital, a very less than excited Dr. Kenny had called and offered his services free of charge…free at least to Jim. Fratto had told him to spare no expense making sure that he was okay.

Charlie had made a call and got the address with a request for an appointment, and it was one he did not have any interest in being late for. When he pulled up to the gate, a team of six guys came out. Not one of them looked as if they'd have any qualms with putting two shots into Charlie's head immediately if he gave them a single excuse to do so.

Charlie, of course, would be absolutely fine if he could avoid such a thing from happening. There were two dogs, each of them had cropped ears and he was pretty sure they were Doberman Pinschers and by the fact that they didn't look like anything he'd ever seen a picture of other than the ears mostly because of the fact that these ones were completely jacked in the muscle department. He could only make a safe assumption that these were probably not from a rescue shelter. One man was walking around with a mirror on a stick and Charlie got to go through a full pat down with a search of the car. Charlie was starting to wonder if maybe there was more going on here than met the eye.

Charlie could appreciate the security, but for the love of God, he was the one, one of the ones anyway, that had kept Fratto alive. Charlie tried making a joke - one that crashed before liftoff just saying, "Guys, you know if you wanted to, you know I could have just walked up to the house. I don't need the car, I'm pretty capable of getting around."

None of the men offered any politeness nor their names, and

about the only thing that one did say was, "Would you like to put a suggestion in our box?"

Charlie just shook his head no. He wasn't too concerned and figured that once Fratto was healed up that he'd be back to his own house. He also thought that the box would be located somewhere near his asshole.

Charlie finally made it through all the security checks and drove the short distance up to a house that would probably meet an NBA star's requirements. He got out and there was already a man standing at the front door. Charlie wasn't sure if he had seen him before but could only assume he was the one in charge of Fratto's security now. Charlie figured the guy stood at six-six or six-eight, he wasn't sure, and that didn't matter because Jesus Christ he was big. Charlie did not want to be impolite, but he was a little timid about shaking hands with this behemoth. The man motioned for him to come there and then to raise his arms and turn around. Charlie joked saying, "Please be gentle with me. This is my first time."

The man said, "You're gonna have to get to know me if you're going to be going and seeing Mr. Fratto on a regular basis. Nobody's going to get to the boss without seeing me first."

"Should I call you new guy, or do you have a name? I don't know how often I'll see him, to be honest. Nothing is really how it appears like it'll be in the Keys."

He nodded and seemed to know what he was talking about. It was a strange and dangerous town and weird shit happened. Probably more often in his world than others. "You can call me Mr. Josh or Mr. Qualls."

Charlie, who had not necessarily thought about the new guy and his job and the implications that the responsibilities carry for the job asked, "So that's a pretty good gig right? I mean getting to be the head guy in charge of Fratto and security and stuff? Oh, and what are the chances of me calling you Josh?"

Mr. Josh shrugged and responded as honestly and quickly as possible without even having to really think about his words and replied, "Slim, very slim. Do you need me to repeat your choices of what you can call me?"

"No, I got it, but this isn't an easy decision. I don't want it to feel like we are uptight towards each other. This isn't easy but how about we start with…Mr. Josh?"

"Kid, I really don't fucking care. But yeah? It's great, it's one of those jobs where you're the first one to take a bullet for your boss. If you don't take a bullet and he lives, he'll put a bullet in you. Best job ever…but we got a dental plan."

"Is this one of those jobs where you probably don't have a lot of choices in saying yes or no?"

Mr. Josh tapped his nose and opened the door, stopping Charlie as he began to walk in with a mitt of a hand on his shoulder saying, "Keep Mr. Fratto calm. Dr Kenny is taking a nap and he said if his blood pressure gets too high that he's going to drug whoever it is that does it and snip their balls off. Do you understand?"

Charlie very much did not want to lose his very beloved although since he'd been in the Keys not very useful manhood. He replied, "I will talk very slowly, and calmly. I promise, do you believe me?"

Mr. Josh shrugged saying, "I don't really give a shit, so long as it isn't my nuts. Don't touch anything and follow me."

Charlie wasn't sure as he followed Mr. Josh that the damn hallway would ever end. He thought maybe if their business did good he might be able to rent one of the bedrooms in the back. He figured if he came back with a girl of questionable morals, and she saw this place that he would have very strong chances of laying vertically . For good measure, Mr. Josh tapped Charlie on the shoulder whispering, "Cut your goddamn balls OFF."

Charlie really didn't think there was anything he was going to say which would upset Fratto. Although he hadn't had too many conversations with him, he felt like, from the ones that he'd had so far, everything had gone okay. Charlie did know very well that pain could wear a person out and having bullet wounds was probably no different. It could also in the right people probably push their tolerance level to being almost impossible to see. Mr. Josh cleared his throat, and Fratto set a book down looking up, taking a drink of tea, and motioning for Charlie to come in. Mr. Josh stood there, apparently not sure if he should stay or go. Fratto stared at him for a good twenty count before Mr. Josh finally asked, never assuming with Mr. Fratto saying, "Did you want me to go, sir?"

Fratto said, "Did you search him? Did I ask you to stay?"

"Yes, yes sir, we did. They searched his car too."

"His car? Did he bring the car inside the house?"

Mr. Josh couldn't have missed the rhetorical question much more. He replied swiftly, "No sir, it wouldn't fit through the…"

"Josh, if you want this to be a long-term gig then you might start thinking with your top head. You can go, and in the future, if I want you to stay, don't worry, I will not be nervous about asking you to do so. I have little worry in life about offending people and saying the wrong thing. Quite frankly, I could give two flying fucks. You know, I feel my blood pressure going up a little bit. Maybe we need to talk to Dr Kenny. Wasn't that part of his orders?"

He instantly turned around, slapping himself in the head as he did, letting everyone know this lesson was learned. Fratto had to hold back a smile and motioned for Charlie to come into the room; he still didn't actually know if this was Dr. Kenny's place or Fratto's or if it was one and the same. Charlie said, "Looking alive, Mr. Fratto."

"You know your Uncle Joe wouldn't bullshit me, Charlie."

Charlie shrugged saying, "Your chest is going up and down. I didn't say you looked good. Just that you look alive. Nothing personal, of course."

Fratto was nodding his head, thinking that the kid was right. He pushed the button on the bed, setting himself up to a little higher angle. Charlie tried to not look at him while he was doing it. He wasn't a doctor, but there was no question if he was in any sort of pain. Fratto said, "What brings you all the way out here, Charlie? I have a feeling that you didn't want to play cards, right?"

Charlie shrugged saying, "Well I have time, which you might not know is part of the reason that I'm here. But the reason that I'm here is because I have time. You'd mentioned I could always reach out for help if I needed it. I think you especially said that after you'd gotten shot and…"

Fratto wasn't necessarily in a bad mood, but he also was still a recovering man dealing with the pain from gunshot wounds. He said, "Charlie, I might not be at a hundred percent, but I assure you my head is just fine. I don't need any reminders of what you did for me and what I said I would do. If I say I'm going to do something, it gets done. Case in point, no one has seen or heard from my son since that night. He was already scooped up and taken out before police could ever show up."

Charlie was nodding, and after a moment of awkward silence, realized that this was his time or turn to talk. Charlie said, "If at any point you start feeling like this conversation is upsetting you, please let me know. It can wait a few more days until you're feeling better."

"Do you know how long recovery time is that I have to fucking deal with, Charlie? If I can go an entire recovery without getting pissed off, it would be a damn near miracle. So, spit it out, kid."

"So, Jim, the redheaded guy that was with me that night that took a bullet, he's feeling great and I'm sure he sends his thanks for getting him taken care of. But, he had made the genius statement that he thought we should open up our own investigation service, you know, to the news station that arrived."

"Well, how many cops do you know that retire and go into some kind of private security work? You know the kind you can actually make good money with?"

"Exactly, so that's kind of what I was talking about. I'm completely okay with doing it even though you know we've never done anything remotely close to that but that's not necessarily what the problem is. I know that wouldn't be one you could solve if I didn't want to do the job either. Other than maybe taking out Jim for me which, no offense to Jim, but some days I don't think would be the worst thing in the world for my patience," Charlie held up his hands, realizing he was rambling to a guy that people did not ramble to and didn't have the patience more than likely to deal with it. Charlie continued, "I'm sure we could do certain things without one. But we all thought, or Tim and I thought, that if we were licensed as well as having the blessing for a permit to carry in case we needed it, that it might just be for the best."

"You said a lot, and at the same time, absolutely nothing."

"I'm trying to get a business license for being a private detective. So are Tim and Jim. As well as the license to carry in a professional manner."

"What's the reason that you haven't been able to get it? I assume you did fill out the forms right or you probably wouldn't come to me as I'm not a fucking secretary."

"No sir, and I would never think of you as one. I did do some research before I even filled the forms out and it looks like a lot of the time you might need the blessing of the local law enforcement to get one."

"So, you're coming to me because let me just guess your thoughts are that Detective Lindvall is currently bending the three of you over. I'd imagine he isn't letting your applications through and over all putting a stranglehold on the process. I'm sure that you know he'd probably never get over that little issue pissing him off."

"Yeah, unfortunately I don't think he likes us very much. I have a feeling that he probably holds us personally responsible for getting a very large portion of his side income stopped from coming in regularly."

"Yeah, it's a shame when you're a cop and you lose your dirty money. Those sports cars, second houses, and girlfriends don't pay for themselves. So, I would imagine he's already tried to find a new avenue to earn. Because it would have been ridiculous had he gotten a job that just paid enough in the first place."

"Yes, that does seem to be the case though. Even as inconvenient as that must be for him."

"And you'd like me to use some of my contacts maybe to be able to push that through?"

"Would that be too much to ask?"

"Absolutely, if I didn't owe you and if I didn't like you and maybe if I hadn't promised your Uncle Joe that I would take care of you if you ever came to the Keys."

Charlie had always been thankful for his Uncle Joe. He definitely knew that his life could have been drastically different if family hadn't been there to take care of him. But, he also had not ever expected his post-naval career to be what it was turning out to be. He'd not really known what was next yet, but doing more things related to being a police officer had not been any of them. Even though it was what had been expected, it had turned out to be a blessing because he had a place to live for as long as he wanted, so long as no one sank his boat. At the same time, it might have been a curse because his friend had gotten shot. The guy that was supposed to look out for him had gotten shot, and he had been locked up in jail, although he'd gotten out or escaped, or you know, something all along those lines. Charlie replied, "But I guess it's a good thing that I check all those boxes, isn't it?"

Fratto apparently wasn't really in a chit chat kind of mood. He looked at Charlie for a second saying, "Is there anything else, Charlie?"

"No sir, If there's anything you need like dropped off or whatever just give me a call, I can help out."

"Oh, I think I've got plenty of people that can do my errand work, but I do appreciate the sentiment."

Charlie didn't want to ask when he was going to make the call because he knew that any time that was sooner than never was going to be better than he could do. Charlie gave a thumbs up saying, "Well we hope you feel better, and it'll be nice when you're all healed up and back to fighting weight.

You look like you've got plenty of security here. But I am curious, what are you so worried about or is this just your wife keeping you safe and at home?"

Fratto moved his pillow again and under it was a pretty similar machine gun shined up like the one he had had that night. There were extra magazines as well as a pistol. He surely realized that chances were definitely strong that he might not think all of this shit was over. But if he had to guess, Charlie didn't think that Fratto would ever be surprised again or lacking hardware. Fratto said, "Well I don't want to dig into it until there's something to worry about. But I figured that it would be smart that I am ready and not surprised. The wife is in the tropics. She isn't coming back until I know that everything around here is as safe as we are used to, at least."

"You are a wise man, sir. Do you know who or if this might fall at my feet?"

"I can't say. But a smart man would keep a piece on him at all times. I don't know that there's going to be retaliation, or requests? They might think this is a time to strike, given my status."

"Good information to have, sir. Thank you for letting me know. Oh, and thanks for taking care of helping me with this. I just feel better about making sure I do things the right way and legally."

Fratto laughed, gripping one of the two spots he'd been shot. He said, "That doesn't feel like it is entirely the legal way to go about it, but I'm not going to cast the first stone. Let me know if you need anything else."

"I will, and thank you for your time, Mr. Fratto. Please get back on your feet sooner than later."

Charlie walked out nodding to Mr. Josh as he walked to his car. He wasn't trying to look at this place with fresh eyes, but to be honest, he couldn't help himself. When he looked around there were definitely more guys walking the perimeter armed to the teeth than was necessary if things were cool. Charlie didn't know if that was because he was being paranoid after being shot at or that things really had gone to hell. He couldn't help but think 'thanks a lot' for the heads-up guy whose life I saved. Charlie drove out slowly, still sure any of these guys made plenty enough not to need to think if shooting anyone and asking questions later was a novel idea.

Charlie still needed to change the presets on the radio but didn't have any issues with Uncle Joe's taste. Charlie could remember his feet dangling off the bench seat of his uncle's old truck. The current pickup was more than either of them would have ever expected to ride in. As a young boy, and even now, Charlie couldn't have cared less if it was a piece of crap. He would trade everything now just to have his Uncle Joe back. He couldn't help but smile and get a little choked up thinking of his uncle with the windows down screaming at the top of his lungs. When Charlie didn't think it could get any louder a pretty girl would be within ear shot and that's when he'd get a lot louder.

After he'd sung two or three songs he realized talking to Fratto and driving around had surprisingly taken considerably less time than he had expected. Charlie hadn't figured he'd need to run through some sort of a gauntlet to be able to get his request done but you never knew. He wasn't dying to get back to the boat. The last thing he'd want to do is wake anyone up. The Jim and Tim duo took a little bit to wake up and not be grumpy. There wasn't much to do with the boat at this point, so they'd just be sitting around and staring at each other or potentially going out for a spin.

They had done a very good job not giving Jim the unnecessary opportunity to get addicted to some very strong painkillers that Kenny had given him. He was a little belligerent after the first time he took two at once only for them to realize with these things that was probably enough for a show horse to take. Tim and Charlie had taken turns keeping a hold of them, giving them half a one every so many hours after calling and talking to the doctor about it. Kenny had advised the two of them were both really shitty at reading directions on labels. The fact that they assumed these were Ibuprofen size power had blindly gone by them. He'd also mentioned that with just having a gunshot wound to the arm that hadn't torn anything too horribly up that they could probably ween him off them after a few weeks. That was definitely something they'd do until Jim had tried to lift something only to tear his muscle and had to go back to the doctor...again. This time it was Kenny who had done the work, letting him know his keepers were blind and he was stupid and that when a doctor says not to lift something, that is exactly what you should do.

Charlie cruised near the docks, wondering what he should do until his stomach seemed to raise its hand and began to gurgle, answering his question for him. He realized not only had he missed breakfast, but he'd missed lunch as well. It's amazing, he always thought, how quickly time could go by when you weren't really all that busy doing anything. Which he always figured was the prime reason that days went by so quickly when you didn't have to work and if you didn't love your job then it was like someone dragging their nails down your back just an inch at a time.

Charlie had to go around the block to find a spot. He was still getting used to the current time of year in the Keys, it definitely had busier times than others. Right now, at the beginning of summer was definitely one of those times. He held the door open for a few people to come out and walked in, remembering back to the first time he'd eaten at Leslie's Place. It was amazing how one month's time could change how busy a place could be. His first dining experience there had been just him and the two owners.

Charlie looked around, trying to find a seat, or better yet, he'd even settle for a stool at the counter. He didn't have any company, so he didn't need a hell of a lot of room. When Leslie saw Charlie she was just wiping up a spot when she yelled above the crowd, "Ford, get your pretty ass over here and sit down before the spot is gone."

Another man who apparently had been looking for a spot snapped, "Well why the hell did you get him a spot and not me?"

"Because I like to look at him. Also, we're friends, and he isn't a tourist. He's a resident. So, his money will last after the summer. I'm sure a spot will open up soon."

"You do realize I could go somewhere else, you stupid fucking lady?"

Charlie set down his newspaper at his spot. He walked over to the guy, who outweighed Charlie of course, which given the man was fat and overweight was not really a big surprise. Charlie probably figured this guy peaked in high school and said, "Why don't you apologize to Leslie here. This is her joint. She's not anything but sweet. Even though she might have her own sense of humor and be a little dirty at times. But it is her place, and she can do pretty much whatever she wants to do."

Mark was busy flipping burgers, grilling steaks and making sure the fries didn't burn and yelled, "Charlie, you want to borrow my meat tenderizer? I got a butcher's knife, hatchets, and all kinds of shit."

Charlie looked the guy up and down saying, "No, I'm alright. I don't think I need it."

Leslie shook her head at her husband yelling, "So nice of you, dear, to stand up for me. I appreciate it. It is hard to beat a man's chivalry nowadays."

"Honey, I'm too pretty to go to jail."

"Oh, you're too something, Mark, definitely something."

Charlie looked back to the man who wasn't reading all those subtle hints. The stranger said, "How about you stick it in your ass, and I'll save the apology and this fucking lady can just find me somewhere to eat. I just want to get some food and get out of here. If you knew who I was, you would know that you probably shouldn't fuck with me. I'm kind of a big deal where I live."

Charlie put a hand on the man's shoulder and said, "I know you think that you're very special and that's really great. But I think your opportunity to eat here, at least under current ownership, has passed. You're really missing out on a great burger and fries or really anything. I think I'm yet to have a bad meal except for the day Mark had the runs and Leslie had to cook."

"I told him we should have shut down for the day. You also know I don't cook except for my delicious pies. So, I feel like it might be both of your guys' faults."

The man shook off Charlie's hand, walking forward and shoving Charlie back with what he could only assume was all of his force available. Charlie shook his head and looked at Leslie. He said, "I can always clean up if I make a mess."

She shrugged, looking at the man, smiling and saying the kindest way to go fuck themselves, "You have a blessed day, sir."

He gave her the finger and Charlie said, "You touch me or give my friend the finger in her own restaurant again and I'm going to make sure that I remove it and stick it up your ass. Oh, and when you finally do get lunch, you'll need to drink it through a straw."

For a moment, the man looked like he was going to turn around but didn't turn his feet enough for Charlie to actually believe him. Pink polo shirt guy came back thinking he was throwing a surprise punch. But Charlie's Spidey sense seemed to know that it was coming. The man was aiming directly for Charlie's face. Charlie stepped to the side of the pink polo guy, who apparently had had no shortage of surprise and confidence because he had, without a doubt, completely missed his target.

He tried to counter the mess up with a left hook again. Charlie always said if you weren't a good drunk, don't drink. If you couldn't cook, then don't invite people over for supper. The most important thing was if you couldn't win a fight, then don't pick one. He wasn't quite sure why someone so sloppy would try to pick a fight in the first place. After he had missed twice, the guy came straight for him, arms wide, and gripped Charlie's shirt. Charlie only had so many shirts with buttons and regardless didn't care either way he didn't want this guy touching him. The pink polo guy had fire in his eyes. Apparently, he thought Charlie should have been scared, but the look was more confusion than anything else. Charlie was questioning what he thought his next move would be because the guy didn't really have a set of extra hands.

Charlie, of course, wasn't going to wait around for the pink polo guy to figure out what he should do if he wanted to have any type of success. Charlie was completely healed up after a month from his original session of getting the shit kicked out of him and wasn't about to have that happen again…not if he could help it, by god. He knew that he should get out of this guy's grip but the only worse thing than someone who couldn't fight was someone who couldn't fight and was absolutely pissed off. Charlie said, "So, were you going to kiss me? I mean what were you going to do now?"

"I'm going to kick your goddamn ass!"

"Yeah again, with what, your hands are a bit busy, and you know, no offense, but you are too fat to lift your leg."

Leslie realized this had been going on all of about twenty seconds and was already tired of this. She didn't want that pretty face beat up, and she didn't want to look at the ugly ass pink polo face. She said, "Charlie, be a dear and let's wrap this up. I got tables ready and quite frankly this is stupid."

Charlie winked and the man wasn't quite sure where to go

with this nor what the young man thought he could do. Charlie smiled and knew he wasn't going to be able to get his hands off of him, the guy's arms were twice as big as his. Charlie said, "Get the door, Leslie."

She was not sure what he was going to do that would make the guy want to leave. Charlie brought up his completely free and capable hands using his left to push into his neck. He started gagging trying to get away from Charlie's fingers which didn't seem like they were going anywhere anytime soon. Charlie would have felt bad if the guy wasn't such a cocky prick. Charlie cupped his hand, swinging it around. Polo thought he was going to punch him in the face. However, that wasn't the case, it was worse…much worse. Charlie struck him with the palm bone in his hand right behind his ear. The strike made the guy's vision go a bit wonky. When he didn't let go, Charlie hit him a second time on the right then the left side. His grip didn't disappear, but it also didn't get any stronger. Charlie wasn't really trying to send him to the morgue so brought up a palm strike, hitting him hard enough to make his teeth click together.

Pink polo guy's eyes rolled back into the rear of his head for just a moment. When they came back, Charlie pushed him backward, not stopping until the two of them were out of the diner. Charlie brought up both arms and pushed out. His grip didn't have much to it. He looked like he was going to take one more punch at Charlie who had to give him some credit. He was an absolute idiot but wasn't about to give up his upper hand. Charlie brought one more punch hard into his nose.

The polo man fell down to his ass, not really paying any mind to his nose, and sat there bleeding down his face and onto his shirt. Charlie looked around; apparently keeping to your own business was a thing because not too much interest was taking place in this guy. A little bit of drizzle was starting to come from the right side of his mouth. Charlie said, "You have a fantastic day. You know, you almost had me."

Polo guy looked up, his eyes going into the back of his head and then back down. Charlie said, "Yeah all you would have had to have done was the opposite of everything you did. And then you probably would have had a chance."

Charlie didn't want to sit outside with a drooling man on the sidewalk. He thought he'd probably be more than safe sitting there in his plaid shorts and pink polo shirt that obviously was probably all the rage on the local golf courses. Charlie was pretty sure he'd probably come down to the Keys especially to use that shirt.

He turned around, walking back into Leslie's place to take his seat. Charlie got a few pats on the back as he made his way through the diner to his still waiting stool. Charlie was never one to pick a fight. But his Uncle Joe had told him from a young age if you're gonna start one then be god damn sure that you are the one that finishes it. Mark yelled through his cooks window saying, "Way to go, Charlie. I had your back if anything went wrong. Free water for everyone!"

People perked up until they realized he'd just said water, he didn't get the popular guy's look. Charlie smiled saying, "Oh Mark, I don't think I've ever felt safer knowing you had my back. Thank you so much. I was just waiting for any moment for you to start throwing hamburgers or steaks at the guy."

Mark shook his head saying, "With the price of beef? Good god no. I had some drumsticks that I overcooked earlier so that I could really throw one of those hard as shit."

Leslie brought over a cup of water and a coffee and said,

"What brings you in today, Charlie? I'd like to sit and flirt all day, but it's kind of a madhouse in here, if you haven't noticed."

Charlie had noticed and said, "You know it'd probably be smart if you guys get some summer help for when it's this busy."

"Yeah, we got a dishwasher now and we have a second waitress as well."

Charlie looked around not seeing her and said, "Well she's doing a hell of a job. Is she taking a smoke break?"

"Eww no, she told me this morning that she had a really important phone call she had to take and I'm pretty sure that's where she went to."

"Good to know."

Leslie pushed the menu towards Charlie asking, "How hungry are you today, my knight in shining armor, who is not my husband."

"I'm not gonna lie, I could eat. I had every intention of getting breakfast today and then lunch, but between taking care of baby Jim and making sure babysitter Tim didn't kill him it's almost like it's a full-time job. I mean, so long as you do not want to get paid for it. Because then that actually probably would be an actual job. I'm starting to think maybe he needs to get charged for all this fantastic care that we've given him."

She said, "Did you want to be a nice friend and take something back for the two of them?"

Charlie shrugged saying, "Well, I guess I could do it anyways. I mean I don't necessarily want them to start thinking that I like them or anything."

Leslie smiled and Charlie ordered four hamburgers, two fries, and two cokes to go and ordered his own food for there. Charlie was thankful that just because they were busy in the summer that they didn't jack up their prices to screw over the working man or working people.

Charlie took a look around the diner, still surprised to see it so damn full. When he opened the newspaper a manila envelope fell down to his feet. Charlie immediately gave another glance around trying to see if anyone was watching him because to his knowledge he had not had a manila envelope when he left today. Charlie pulled it up, placed it in front of him and tapped the guy sitting next to him on the shoulder saying, "Hey buddy, do you know who put this envelope here? I mean are they still here?"

He shrugged a non-committal but said, "No clue, partner, I was watching you messing around with the dipshit in the pink polo. I've never been a big fan myself of fighting, but it's got to hurt using your damn palm on someone's face doesn't it?"

Charlie replied, "It's not that bad. I mean it's not necessarily pleasant. But it also hurts worse on the receiver of it."

The man could see Charlie's point but still wasn't sold on the aspect of something that could break his hand by using it as a makeshift battering ram weapon. Charlie didn't know if he should open up that envelope inside. He didn't think that there would be anything too horrific in there but at the same time didn't want any onlookers asking any questions that he either didn't feel comfortable with or have any interest in entertaining the idea of having the answer to.

Charlie was halfway through his meal when a waitress walked in front of him grabbing a pitcher of coffee to do refills on her tables. He'd been pretty focused on just the food, but the woman walked right past him and had just a little shake in her step and he could not deny the fact that even though he wasn't trying to gawk that she definitely caught his attention. She had his gaze until she had disappeared heading to the other tables.

Charlie looked up and saw Mark smiling, giving him a wink. Apparently, it was one of those guy code things where everyone realized that she looked damn good. Unfortunately, nowadays it could be a little difficult mentioning that to someone, given the fact that it could be taken in a million wrong ways. It also didn't help a very simple fact which was that he really hoped her pronouns were all the ones that he preferred, and he was her ideal candidate as well.

Leslie came by seeing Charlie's envelope and said, "Is that for me?"

Charlie looked at it, flipping it over and actually seeing lightly written in a pen the letters C F on it and he showed her saying, "No, this looks like it's for me, Leslie."

Leslie snapped her fingers replying, "Damn it. I wish that was going to be my winning lotto ticket, but it doesn't look like that's the case. What a crock of shit. I guess running away with some young hot thing and leaving Mark here to wonder what could have been, is gonna have to just wait for another day."

Charlie smiled; it was impossible not to smile when Leslie was giving her husband shit. It cracked his ass up in every way possible and he loved it. Charlie replied, "If I hit the lotto, Leslie, I'll make sure I give you a good million, and that way you can be a sugar mama for as you say, 'some young thing'."

Leslie put both hands to her heart smiling, fanning herself a little bit. Mark yelled from the window, "You know I heard that, right? I hear everything. Nothing gets past me."

Leslie looked over her shoulder smiling saying, "Yes dear, I know that you heard because I wanted you to. I just hope that you won't miss me too badly when I'm on some lovely tropical island where the water is clear, the sand is warm, and the drinks are as strong as my young thing is har…"

"For the love of God, woman! Would you please be quiet? Good God, I think you're worse now than when we got married."

Leslie knew she could continue taunting him until the cows came home but figured it would probably be best to let him focus on his cooking. She didn't want the orders getting backed up because that was when skinny tips started coming which no one in the food industry whatsoever enjoyed or appreciated. When the new waitress came by, Charlie was trying to do his best not to look this time. Leslie yelled, "Hey Candace, come here real quick. Let me introduce you to this young fine-looking piece of ass that's a regular here."

Charlie was not a hundred percent sure, but he felt more than confident that his jaw had just dropped a foot slamming off of their counter. He could imagine somebody sitting there with a hand crank getting his jaw back where it belonged. If there was one thing he could guarantee from his friend Leslie it was that she could always make his face turn multiple shades of red. The woman definitely had zero issues embarrassing the hell out of him. He was pretty sure that she might be the devil in disguise.

Charlie noticed he was not the only one whose cheeks went more than a little bit red. Getting used to Leslie was not an overnight ordeal. Mark might possibly deserve to be put in for sainthood. Candace came over, glad that she was not the fine piece of ass being mentioned in this conversation. Candace tried to smile. Charlie noticed her cheeks were red, but her eyes were puffy, and he assumed that the phone call she had been hoping for had either been good news that made her cry, or bad news which had done the opposite, Charlie wasn't a glass half empty kind of guy, but he didn't assume the best either. Charlie realized he must have been quite the celebrity to Leslie given the fact that Candace walked up wiping off her hand saying, "You must be Charlie."

Charlie nodded saying, "Oh, she doesn't talk about my constituents?"

Candace who obviously paid attention when Leslie talked replied, "Oh, she talks about all three of you. But you definitely don't have red hair so you aren't Jim, and no offense you could tan for a year and probably not beat Tim, if you know what I mean?"

Charlie gasped, grabbing his chest saying, "Are you trying to say that I'm not African American?"

She tapped her nose giving a thumbs up and said, "I hate to break it to you. She didn't really introduce me. My name is Candace. I'll be here for the summer, maybe a little longer if it stays busy. Otherwise, I might have to start looking for something else."

"So, are you a native of the Keys?"

She smiled, saying, "More like a captive, I think."

Leslie, always plentiful with patience, said, "Why don't you get to the point, honey, and maybe see if he can help you? I would be amazed if he were to turn you down. He's a sucker when it comes to hot things like us."

Charlie had adamantly made sure Leslie was well aware that he wasn't starting any business until he had his license. He could assume confidently that she had completely and utterly ignored every single fucking thing he had told her. He wasn't actually sure why he was surprised because she didn't really ever listen to anything that he said. He was pretty sure that

Mark felt the same way about his wife more than likely though it would be considerably more than how Charlie felt.

Charlie said, "I'm not or we're not actually open, just yet. I mean we're getting people's info and everything. But I haven't gotten my license yet."

Candace smiled looking embarrassed and kind of upset that she felt like she'd wasted his time. Charlie did not want that to be how this conversation ended and said, "Well, you never know. I mean I could get my license any day now. What is it that you were looking to hire to have done? I bet I could put ya on the top of our list."

Candace looked like she'd felt a little sigh of relief before saying, "I have a hit that I need to put out on someone." Charlie was just about ready to say something when the two women could not help but bust out laughing. Leslie elbowed her probably a little harder than she should have saying, "See, I told you he was gullible. God, that was worth every damn second of not giving that away."

Candace said, "I'm so sorry. She said that it would make me asking, for what I actually need a lot less awkward."

Charlie smiled, knowing having women in his life would always keep him humble. Charlie said, "Very cute, so what exactly was it that you actually needed done?"

Charlie could see a few tears forming in her eyes and he was just waiting, hoping that the levee wouldn't break. He said, "You don't have to talk about it if you don't want to."

She smiled saying, "It would be somewhat difficult for you to say yes or no if you didn't know what it was that I needed."

Charlie was really starting to like this lady. He said, "Are you sure you shouldn't be like a lawyer or accountant?"

Leslie snapped, saying, "What the hell does that mean?"

Charlie said, "You own your own business, Leslie. I mean you're not really a waitress and trust me I have nothing but the highest respect for people that bring me my food which keeps me from having to cook on a daily basis. I just meant she seems really smart."

Leslie nudged her again saying, "I swear to God I could do this all day long."

Mark yelled from behind her making her jump, "Hey sweet cheeks, get that damn food out and get it delivered. People are gonna start getting pissed off that it's cold. They're gonna blame me because you're going to tell him the cook was slow."

"Well, I don't want them thinking that I'm a bad waitress."

Mark didn't say anything else. Charlie could see both veins pumping in his sweat covered forehead. Leslie took the hint leaving the two by themselves and before long came out with an incredible amount of food balanced down one arm impeccably, not having the slightest hesitation in her step.

Candace said, "It's my ex-boyfriend. I mean, we really only went out a few times. But you could say that he's a little clingy. He didn't necessarily have the same feelings about breaking up with me that I did for him."

"So, you have a stalker or a boyfriend that won't leave you alone?"

"Yes."

"And what is it exactly that you wanted to hire me to do? If you're not looking to hire me for a hit or whatever."

She replied, "Well I was hoping maybe you could get the evidence that I need to prove that he is stalking me and not following the temporary restraining order that I had filed on him. He had said that he's a big enough name down here that he doesn't need to listen to anything that police say. That no one will try to stop him."

Charlie shrugged saying, "Sounds like a real gem. Please don't tell me that he is a cop."

"Oh no, he's not a police officer. It's worse."

"Candace, you're really selling me on taking this job. Let me guess, he's a crooked FBI agent?"

She quite frankly wanted to crawl under a rock. She'd always considered herself a very strong and independent woman but having to do this was not helping her self-esteem in the least, "No, thank god. So, there is a local training gym here. It is called Knuckles and Throws Gym and they train MMA fighters. Like on the professional level."

Charlie could feel the start of a horrible decision. He was already adamantly saying no in his head. He'd said it at least fifty times in just a matter of a few seconds. When he opened his mouth to talk he said, "I could probably help you out with that. I mean you just need some pictures of him not following the court's temporary restraining order, right?"

"Yes, my lawyer, who didn't sound like he wanted to get anywhere within a mile of this, told me no. He said his guys were too good and they wouldn't be stupid enough to follow around someone who beats the shit, excuse my French, out of people for a living."

"Yeah wow, what a bunch of idiots, French excused. I mean, who wouldn't want to follow around someone who trains people to hurt others on purpose."

"Well, it isn't actually that he trains people…"

Charlie had now told himself at least a thousand times that he was an absolute fucking moron. He told himself this wasn't a conversation that you should even be having with anyone yet, guy who doesn't have a license. Guy who would be going after another guy that hangs out with a bunch of guys who probably could kick the absolute shit out of Charlie and his guys. Charlie, hoping…or more so praying that his question was right, "So, he's a promoter or manager?"

"I don't know which belt it is, but he is the current contender for it. He's in this insane training regimen right now. I don't think he'd have time to see me, sleep, and workout at the gym that much."

"Nice to know that he is committed. But to be clear, all I need to do is follow him around?"

"Pretty much. On the off chance you might see him trying to kill me, could you call the police? But be sure to get a picture or video first."

"I'll do a hell of a lot more than that, Candace."

"You can try but can you please call the cops before you come over to try and help."

"You don't think a guy beating the hell out of you isn't a good thing to have stopped asap?"

"Okay, well run to me while dialing 911. They'll trace your phone and hopefully show up within a time that one of us is still able to get the medical care that we need to keep us alive. I know I'm selling the hell out of this job, but I really do need your help. So, I just need to know if I can trust you, Mr. Charlie Ford?"

That voice in his head was saying, 'you won't listen anyway, dickhead.' Charlie replied saying, "Well…I had some pretty easy cases, like a bunch of really not violent ones lined up. I'm not going to lie, having to worry about the cops showing up in time to make sure we both get the medical attention needed to live is going to make a statement on my resume. But there's one request that I'm not going to budge on if we are going to work together…or if I'm going to work for you, to be more accurate."

Candace leaned forward whispering, "What is it?"

"If we end up in the hospital and we are in the same room, I feel like if you get cherry jello and I get orange that you should trade with me. The same can be said with chocolate versus getting vanilla pudding."

She smiled and Charlie, who could usually hold his emotions in check, felt actual pain in his cheeks. He was trying not to but couldn't hold the laughs back. He liked this woman, and he didn't want anything bad to happen to her. There wasn't a lot to do other than being careful. Candace asked, "How much do you charge? I can pay, but I'm not rich by any means."

Charlie shrugged saying, "It'll depend on how much work I need to do as far as the bill. If you want me to do like a three-day thing I'll cut my per price to a set fee. I can give you the piece of crap following you around discount."

"You don't really need to give me any special treatment if you don't want to. I'm not going to turn down a chance to get a lil' extra in my pocket, especially if he kills you and I really need to move."

Charlie gave her a straight face, not really sure what he should say next. He replied, "Hey, I'll need my Yelp reviews to be good. Having your face on there couldn't hurt anything, right?"

Just when she thought her blushing had gone away, which coincidentally had begun when Leslie left, she felt it again asking, "When can you start?"

"I'll need to go back to my office and get a few things. We got a pretty good camera with a zoom lens. I think getting any angles with the two of you as far as him being in the same shot being creepy would work. If we have multiple places with that then I'd think we are okay. They can only deny so much proof, right?"

"Charlie, did you take the job?" Leslie yelled.

"Yeah, I am going to try and help out."

"Good, then figure out what you need and get to work. Candace, I'm glad that I was able to introduce the two of you so that we get this figured out. But if you see that lady in the corner then you can tell if she doesn't get her double ham and cheese with a side of crinkle cut fries that she's going to absolutely lose her shit in the worst way. Oh, and don't forget her ranch…she must be visiting from Iowa or Minnesota."

Charlie scribbled down his number saying, "Do me a favor. Send me a picture of him as soon as you get a chance. It'll make it easier trying to see which guy following you is the one we need pictures of."

"Oh god, don't even joke about more than one stalker. That is terrifying. I'll get you the picture soon. Thank you, Charlie, I really, really appreciate this."

"Happy to help. That's why I'm doing this- to help people."

Candace tucked her paper with the number in her apron and came out looking like a younger version of Leslie carrying a lot of food. He watched her as she delivered the food and that dumb smile that he was pretty sure was painted across his face began to melt away as if it was never there. A man who was sitting on the hood of a car drinking from a gallon water jug made him think there were a lot of telltale signs saying this guy might be her stalker. Charlie got the boys' food and headed out, dying to know what was in the mystery envelope.

Charlie was already running through what needed to be done. He was well aware that people got better at things that they did in repetition. So, for him, he knew this was something that he would get better at over time. However, there was no reason why he should make her get shittier service because of how green he was. Charlie didn't do anything half ass, so when it would be time to work he'd think it out and try to not screw up anything.

Charlie still didn't know who the guy was on the car hood but gave off the idea that until he knew this was the guy that he probably shouldn't fuck with him. One thing that Charlie noticed quickly was that the guy thought Charlie was someone he wasn't worried about fucking with but was curious if he should have been worried about. Unfortunately, when he headed out and looked over he noticed Mr. Pink shirt guy was chatting it up with two gents that didn't scream that they were someone who would hang out with pink shirt guy.

He was obviously pissed, and Charlie could care less if someone was black, pink, or a million other color combinations. But these two guys who were nodding pulling out a folded bank roll, that he was confident were all Benjamins, handed over an additional small handful to him. He knew Columbians were a very dark brown mixed with some Hispanic features. These guys fit the bill. He had to guess they had paid him to be a diversion, maybe so they could put the letter in his paper. He felt like that sounded like a lot of shit to deal with at once and was overkill.

When they saw Charlie walking quickly in their direction the three of them slid into a car and sped off. By the time Charlie thought about his truck in comparison to where he was and knew he could take off at his fastest following the truck or going back after his own. There weren't a lot of options, and he mostly despised the ones that he did have. If he had Jim and Tim then he could have split them into two different cars leaving them to take turns following so they didn't get made.

Charlie slowed down into an angry Olympic speed walker for a second longer before he realized that he probably wouldn't catch up to them. Also, that he probably couldn't have looked like a bigger douche running with his bags of food in his hands. Charlie felt defeated as he started the trek back to the pickup. By the time he got there, the man on the hood and his car were gone as well. Charlie looked at his truck sitting at more of a tripod angle. He looked at the rear tire, seeing a knife through it with a note saying, 'stay away from Candace or I will kill you.'

Charlie set the bags in the car and took off his dress shirt and put the truck on a jack and started breaking free the lug nuts. Charlie, even in death, couldn't give his Uncle Joe any shit…well, he thought maybe could think of a few things to say but they wouldn't be about the truck. By the time he got the tire switched out and climbed back into the truck, he was starting to wonder what would be said about his meals which he'd gotten with only good intentions.

Charlie started the air conditioning and could feel that lovely humidity with his white undershirt wallpapered onto his back. This wasn't a horrible thing, but he'd been more comfortable. Charlie pulled the envelope open and checked the contents. A lone picture fell out of it. He picked it back up with a set of tweezers he had on his Swiss army knife. The last thing he needed was to be killed and the only fingerprints on the evidence was to be his own. Charlie looked around making damn sure that there weren't going to be any people coming up from his sides and smashing through his window and drugging him. Charlie flipped over the picture, dropping it in his lap and speeding off like a bat out of hell.

Chapter 5

Fratto was sitting on the side of his bed. He had his phone in one hand and was using a stress ball in the other which right now looked like it was going to pop in half. He said, "I let a lot of shit go in the Keys that I don't have to turn a blind eye to."

The mayor of the town didn't want to ask exactly what he meant. If Fratto said it then it probably meant that he had proof, pictures, videos, and so much more that he didn't want to know about. The mayor replied, "So exactly what is it that I can do for you, Mr. Fratto? I heard you were injured a month ago but hadn't heard much more."

"Look, I'm calling for one thing and it doesn't have shit to do with my health. Just know that as long as I'm alive, the Keys are going to be mine. Your title has nothing to do with who runs this town. I have every intention of keeping it that way, and if anyone else gets in my way I am going to come at them like I have a fucking sledgehammer to their face."

"So, what could I do for you, today?"

"I need to have some paperwork pushed through."

"Building permit?"

"Did I say I needed a building permit?"

"No, you didn't. What can I help you get Mr. Fratto?"

"Private detective's license."

"Sir, I don't have anything to do with those, it's a police issue. They sign off."

"Then fucking call someone and do it. You got a detective who may or may not like the boys that I'm trying to push this through for. You get it done, don't fuck around and that's all there is to it. If you have an issue with it then get over it because I don't care!"

"But…"

Dr. Kenny snapped at Fratto. He was about the only one besides his wife that could in the world. You didn't piss off the man that kept you alive. Kenny was watching Fratto's heart monitor and feeling concerned. He showed him a needle mouthing, "If you don't settle down, I'm going to jab this needle into your ass. Do you have any questions about that?"

Fratto who was used to people bending to his every whim put his hand over the receiver yelling, "Do you know who you're fucking talking to? Are you seriously threatening me, for the love of God?"

Kenny shook his head no and as Fratto looked like he was deflating a little bit in a calm voice said, "I'm not threatening you with anything because if you don't relax then I can assure you it isn't a threat. It's a goddamn promise that I'm gonna put this little needle in your big ass and then after you pass out, I'm gonna go have a fucking drink. So, keep it up, don't keep it up, I could go for a drink, so if you're feeling lucky..."

Fratto stopped talking, didn't respond and did some breathing exercises that he had learned from a coach that his wife had brought in after he'd had his first heart attack. He had to admit that the exercises did work when done properly. Of course, he couldn't really thank the coach that had come over because anyone knowing that he had any sort of weakness was one person too many. Or he thought maybe two people was too many because he didn't think it was such a great idea to murder his wife.

After Fratto had gotten his breathing and heart rate down, Kenny put the cap back on the syringe. That actually made his heart rate drop another five beats per minute. Fratto put the phone back up to his ear as the mayor was screaming, "I didn't threaten you! I didn't threaten you! I'm not doing anything to you. You just, you…I got the name Charlie Ford and his friends. I'll make it happen. Is there anything else I can do for you?"

Fratto realized immediately that there wasn't really a way to cover the headsets. The mayor asked, "How soon did you want me to get this done? "

Fratto could not say that he necessarily felt bad. It took a lot for him to get that way, and after a month of coming to terms with his son needing to be removed from the world and society, he thought the last thing he was going to do was find another reason to apologize to someone. Fratto was of the firm belief that when you got the answer you needed, or wanted, you would stop talking. You hang up. You don't say anything else, and that conversation is over with. He felt no different about this and hit end on the phone feeling pretty goddamn good about himself. Kenny said, "You going into the detective business with the Ford kid?"

"Hell no, I need one more business like I need another fucking gunshot wound. The detective down at the Keys Police Department has a hard on for trying to make sure these guys can't get anything passed through. I just thought maybe I could grease the wheels for the kid given the fact that I wouldn't be sitting here if I hadn't had him around. He also, of course, had given me all the info I needed to not get killed when that prick of a driver thought it would be an ideal time to try and shoot me."

"So, if your heart rate is going to remain level and you're not going to get upset, I'm going to go have that whiskey. Thanks for giving me all that credit for keeping you from dying. "

Fratto said, "I pay you; I don't have to give my thanks. Why don't you make that drink a double?"

Kenny walked over to the bar, getting two glass tumblers, and filled each with about a half inch of whiskey, smiling, smelling it, and then emptying the contents of what would have been for Fratto's drink into his own. Kenny said, "You're not near healthy enough to start boozing it up, Mr. Fratto. But hell, if you want a guaranteed nap, I still got that shot? Only pinch for a second. How's that sound?"

"Sounds like I'm gonna go back to reading my book. The only shot I wanted was going to be liquid and it would be ingested, not injected."

Chapter 6

The mayor wasted no time calling the police precinct. He got the front desk clerk and immediately asked to be connected to Detective Lindvall. The detective figured maybe the mayor had a hot tip or even better had a favor that maybe he needed taken care of. Lindvall wasn't necessarily an optimist, but he hadn't really had any issues with the mayor before today. Not that he knew the mayor was probably going to shit on his parade.

Lindvall tried to start with the pleasantries saying, "How goes it, Mr. Mayor? Are you still fighting the good fight to make the Keys the coolest place in Florida to be?"

Lindvall knew immediately when the mayor didn't joke at all and said, "Unfortunately that's not what I'm calling for today, Lindvall. I need you to do something for me and that it just needs to be done. There's no if, ands, or buts about it. I just need you to do it."

"How often do I tell you no?"

"Never. It's probably part of the reason why the two of us get along so well."

"I won't lie, your tone kind of made me a little nervous, sir. What exactly is it that needs to be done?"

"Well, what if I told you but it might be dangerous?"

"I'd say the exact same thing. What is it that needs to be done?"

"You know when you guys get forms in and it's your responsibility to review them and make sure that they get signed off on appropriately? As far as whether they deserve it or not?"

Lindvall didn't get an obscene number of requests for the licenses in the first place. He definitely got requests from honest citizens at least about getting permits to carry. Not the detective part so much. He knew exactly who the mayor was most likely talking about. The mayor put his fears in stone and said, "It's for a Charlie or Charles Ford and if the application is not for just himself and it has two other gentlemen on it just push it through. Otherwise, I need you to figure out what the other guy's names are and do the same thing."

"Sir, this seems a little bit below, much below, painfully below your pay grade. Can I ask what reason there is that you decided to put this task on yourself? I'm just saying I think that you probably have more important things to worry about than a stupid detective's license. I mean, it's just a glorified way to say it's okay to go and stalk people."

"I don't necessarily feel like I need to explain myself to you, Lindvall. Now is this going to be an issue or is it something that you can just take care of? You've always been my go-to and I don't really see any reason why that needs to end now. I'm sure there's no up-and-coming fellow officers that would be interested in what you do taking your spot. What do you have to say about that?"

"I would say that Charlie Ford has got himself some powerful friends in powerful places."

"Yeah, it would sure as hell seem like it looks that way doesn't it?"

"When did you want to have this completed by? "

The mayor who still thought his life was being threatened snapped screaming, "You're not already looking for the fucking form? Get off your ass and go find those goddamn forms and get them to whoever the fuck they need to go to. Let them know that this is per the mayor! There is no screwing around, no bureaucratic red tape. It gets done today. Do you understand, Lindvall?"

"Yeah, I understand. Of course, I don't like it…but I'm sure nobody gives a shit."

"Charlie or possibly Charles Ford. There could be three of them, there could be one. Find them, push them through and get it done immediately."

"Is this an alias?"

"Jesus Christ, this is me telling you what to do. You figuring it out, and then it happens."

"See, you're not dumb. It's why you're my go to Detective. Now get this done for me, please, and I'll make sure and take care of you the next time something comes up that maybe you could help out with."

Lindvall hung up the phone. He didn't have to look for Charlie's and the others' paperwork. He had a special pile for things that needed someone in the police force to sign off on in a little drawer labeled 'Go fuck yourself it ain't ever gonna happen.' Charlie had a stack of the original paperwork at the top. Lindvall could feel his stomach turning with absolute annoyance that this skinny prick was going to get his way. Apparently, it didn't matter if someone had been sent to jail recently; they could still get a detective's license and a permit to carry. Lindvall of course ignored the fact heavily that he had been the one to take them to jail, and he had also been the one to do everything under false pretenses. So, he took the form, stamping **Approved** on it and walked it down to the correct person who was competent and let them know it was a rush job.

Lindvall sat at his desk thinking and realizing, what would happen if he caught him before he got the license? The mayor could not be upset if he was doing his job and Charlie was working outside of the law, could he? This was all something that he was praying he could catch him doing. He knew he'd have to catch him in the act because no one with any common sense would possibly narc on themselves.

Chapter 7

Charlie was going for broke. He didn't think that there was
much reason to slow down. When he'd seen that photo, it put
his ass in gear. He wasn't one to mess around, but when
things felt like they were on the wire, it was a hurry that most
didn't understand. Charlie knew that there was a certain
statement being made by having a picture dropped off with
no explanation and nothing else. If it hadn't been his friends,
Charlie might have been impressed with the timing and
thought that had gone into something like this. There was a
finesse about it that he really didn't care for.

Charlie was driving like an absolute crazy son of a bitch.
Which was not necessarily something he normally did. But,
when your two best friends are in the picture both sleeping
with a gun barrel inches away from their heads you didn't
fuck around. He had to question if good things were going on
right now. Charlie was leaning towards no. He didn't have to
drive too far because Leslie's Diner wasn't far from where the
boat stayed.

Charlie was taking the corners, barely slowing down. The tires
barked in the back as he fishtailed, punching the engine, not

giving it a second to breathe. He was not super excited about the prospect that he could get pulled over on the way there, but at the same time figured the chances of getting stopped were pretty goddamn slim. An additional issue that he was currently debating was what he would do when he got there. The upper hand was definitely not his at the moment.

Charlie had one of the pistols from his gun buying splurge after his ass beating. But the fact that the barrel in the picture had a silencer on it meant that he probably wasn't dealing with any rookies. Charlie was having somewhat of a sick feeling in his gut as he thought about Fratto and his entire crew seemingly on guard and protecting, not looking like they were taking it easy at all. Charlie thought he might need to have a conversation with him about possibly letting him know if his life was in danger a little earlier. Charlie didn't think that was too much to ask, given the simple fact that he had done basically the same thing for Fratto. If Charlie had waited just a few minutes longer, he probably would have been dead.

Charlie pulled in going like a bat out of hell into the parking lot. The same one that still had burn marks from where Jim and Tim's truck had gone up in a fiery explosive blaze. Charlie hit the brakes, sliding to a stop. He didn't waste any time getting out and taking off in a run. Bystanders watched and knew exactly who he was. Charlie was racing down to the slip he kept his boat in with a pistol out and ready and by his side. Charlie figured even after a moderately calm month that they were not going to be earning neighbor of the year awards anytime soon. There was no shortage of fun when the three of them were around. Charlie was racing like a bat out of hell and Johnney stuck his head out the window yelling, "Hey, you tell your friends that these slips are just for us. If they're not paying for them they're not using them. There's plenty of other docks out there that they can use."

Hearing that didn't make him feel any better. It also didn't make any sense on account of them not really having any friends. Charlie was going to ask what kind of boat it was but figured shoot first and get details later. Johnney wasn't a slouch and knew right away with the amount of effort he was putting into his run mixed with the shiny Beretta by his side that he was running with a purpose, having been a previous part of their group, he had a pretty good idea that without question there was something foul here.

Charlie checked over his shoulder, not too surprised when he saw Johnney pulling down a 12-gauge pump and setting it on his counter. He wasn't about to have any repeats of hiding and worrying about dying like a month ago. Charlie liked the idea of having backup, except technically to have backup Johnney would have had to leave his shack. However, he was currently closing the chain rolling security system he had installed on his own dime, which would keep anyone from putting a hand through his little shack. However, it was a perfect size to put the barrel of a shotgun through, which was his current gun of choice.

Charlie's heart was racing as he took two long strides and jumped up into the air going over the railing of the boat realizing he was about as loud as a bull in a China shop. When he made it there, the door to the boat was already open. Charlie had to use his willpower when he made it into the little kitchen area of the boat, not quite expecting to see what he thought he would.

Nydegger was sitting at the recently replaced kitchen table. Charlie was already livid about everything going on but could see his legs shaking crazily. If he was nervous it was not a difficult conclusion to come up with. He did notice that Nydegger was not quite the man that he had once been. He had definitely recently had the shit kicked out of him and noticed if he was going to go pinky ring shopping it would only be for one. He had a fresh bandage wrapped around his palm on his left hand. Charlie hoped that that didn't have anything to do with him or his own future. He was super okay with the fact that it probably hurt. But keeping all five of his fingers on each hand would be ideal.

Charlie, being the eloquent speaker which he was, asked, "What the fuck are you doing on my boat? You realize the last time we talked, you had me fucking arrested? Because of your fucking people, my uncle died. Give me one good reason why I shouldn't shoot you in the face; no sorry, shoot you repeatedly in the fucking face, Nydegger."

"I suppose my pain and discomfort would not be a valid reason?"

Charlie pulled the hammer back on the pistol as Nydegger put up both hands saying, "Kidding, kidding, kidding, I know we've had a less than stellar relationship."

"Yeah, that might be the easiest way to say that. Now get with it before I start firing, I'm not fucking around. Tell me right now where Jim and Tim are?"

"I told them that you were not going to be happy. I did, and did anybody listen to me? Hell no, they didn't. They said they didn't give a shit if you were happy or not. I told them that you weren't really a guy that they wanted on their bad side."

"Well, it seems that they were smarter than you since they didn't come here themselves. Now again where are Jim and Tim?"

"Not here, but they didn't tell me where they were going. Can you put the gun away and sit down so we can talk please? I swear to God, I will not fuck you around, and it isn't a trick."

Charlie kept the gun on Nydegger and walked around, looking in the three rooms, making sure that there wasn't anyone who thought they would surprise Charlie. When he felt at ease about that went back to the table making sure all his bases were covered. Nydegger had his hands up already, but Charlie reached in, gripping the pudgy lawyer by the back of the neck, and ripped him out of his seat. Before Nydegger could say anything, Charlie had kicked his feet apart eand pushed him gut first onto the dinette tabletop. When he tried to push himself up, Charlie had put the gun in his waistband, freeing his hand. Charlie didn't hold anything back when he lifted and proceeded to slam Nydegger face first into the very hard table. Needless to say, Nydegger did not make an attempt to push back up off the table a second time.

Charlie highly doubted the prick had some sort of weapon on him, but he also hadn't thought there'd be a picture of his two friends with guns to their heads left in a paper while he was trying to have a late lunch. He pulled Nydegger back up and threw him headfirst into his seat where he connected with the side of the boat. Charlie waited for Nydegger to straighten himself in his seat before sitting down himself across where he put down the gun on its side, still pointed firmly at Nydegger's chest. Nydegger asked quiveringly a second time, "Could you please put the gun away? They make me so nervous."

Charlie didn't even give a hint of a smile replying, "Nydegger, I can do a lot of things. I could put the gun away or I could keep it out. I could shoot you in the face or again I could not. I have endless options at hand. The options I'm picking are if I don't get a fucking answer that I want in the next thirty seconds, I'm going to shoot you and I'm going to continue shooting you until you tell me one goddamn thing that makes me not want to shoot you. Please keep in mind that it would take a lot to not want to kill you."

Nydegger's face was turning white. But he was quite confident Charlie could give two flying F's how he felt or what he was thinking. He said, "Did you get the picture?"

Charlie nodded saying, "Yeah, did you guys by chance plant someone in there to try and pick a fight with me? Was that your idea?"

"I had a feeling that you might stand up for Leslie in a time of need. We were trying to keep things, you know, on the down low until we were able to make sure everything had gone as planned."

Right now, Charlie was wishing that they hadn't replaced the table so quickly after he'd broken it when dealing with Bruno and Lou and said crew. The idea of reaching across, grabbing him by the neck, and then squeezing until all signs of life ceased to run through his veins gave him a euphoric feeling. Charlie asked, "So what the fuck do you want?"

Nydegger said, "The men that took them are who tried to get

Fratto's son, Junior, to take over the Keys. They knew if he was in charge, people would leave them alone. But you and your friends kind of fucked all that up…didn't you?"

Charlie aimed his pistol, firing once lodging a bullet in the expensive mahogany backrest and effectively scaring the absolute piss quite literally out of Nydegger. He screamed, "You almost hit me. You almost hit me!"

"I told you I was gonna shoot you in thirty seconds if you didn't tell me something good. As of now all you've told me is shit that I don't fucking care about."

"Well, you should care about it, because if you don't do what they say then…"

"Let me guess, Jim and Tim are dead?"

"Cliché, right? I told them the same thing."

"Who are they, or them?"

"You know every gangster in the world?"

"No…"

"Then, just call them the Smith gang."

"Really, the Smith gang?"

"Charlie, you can't look it up online. It isn't like there's a website. I thought you were smarter than…"

Charlie held the gun up pointing it about two inches from Nydegger's nose. Surprisingly enough it completely shut him up. Charlie said, "So, get to it. Obviously, I got something to do soon."

"So, part of your uncle getting taken out was just the first part of a plan. Then there was Fratto, junior taking over and…"

He slammed his free hand on the table making it shake, "Nydegger, please bring up my uncle again. I have a feeling that everything I need is sitting right there in front of you. Is that right?"

Nydegger was confident…like really confident that he could feel his balls going up slowly into his throat. Charlie watched as his face visibly began to turn green. He would have felt bad if it wasn't for him being an absolute piece of shit scumbag lawyer that was more than responsible for his uncle getting killed. He handed over the envelope saying again, "I swear to God I was out of this. I wasn't going to do any more of it. I didn't want anything to do with this in the first place. I just wanted to be one of the unethical backstabbing people screwing over lawyers…like the rest of them, damn it. Is that too much to ask, is that such a bad life?"

"Ethically you mean?"

Nydegger slid over the envelope. Right now, Charlie could tell he wasn't one of the happiest men on Earth. Nydegger said, "So, the details are in here but the gist of it is they had planned to have this boat and a few other boats under Fratto's employment. Obviously, this boat wasn't the only one in the entire network he used; that would be silly. But, if they don't get this delivery made then there's going to be some serious issues coming back this way."

"Is this where the Jim and Tim die thing comes into play if I don't do it?"

"That is definitely a strong probability. I wouldn't have anything to do with that, other than giving you the info. I don't know that I'm going to be needed for anything else."

"Well, we can only hope that when they're done with someone and don't need them anymore that they get rid of them," Nydegger had been doing accounting in his head ever since the men had met him at his office, and forced him to go with them, and the head honcho in charge had cut his finger off. He had a pretty strong idea what his current liquid assets looked like and had seriously debated how far and how quickly he could get out of the Keys and go somewhere preferably without a hard process of getting a visa to live there and as well that also had a very very strict and thorough law against drugs, gangs, smuggling, and most importantly for Nydegger, killing citizens…old and new with a side of not being forced to be sent back to America.

Nydegger responded, "Yes, we will have to see how they feel about keeping people around that they would, I can only pray, no longer have any interest in working with after the job has been done."

Charlie reached across, grabbing the paperwork, figuring it'd be best if he didn't have any questions on something that was a life and death situation. Charlie looked, seeing the GPS coordinates, and realized he'd probably need something to figure out where the fuck those were. The last thing he wanted to do was type in those coordinates on his own personal phone. He didn't know why that was such a bad idea but just figured to be on the safe side that it probably was not intelligent. He looked up at Nydegger saying, "So am I meeting a boat or am I meeting a person on land?"

Nydegger shrugged and he said, "I don't know, but they said that you have twelve hours to get this done."

Charlie looked at his clock trying to think on his feet. He knew that lying was wrong but lying to Nydegger was less of an issue for him. Charlie said the best thing he could think of, "So, they know that I needed to get the engines on the boat fixed? We chunked a few pieces of wood when we were out well, Johnney hit a few pieces of wood while they were out and on their way to come and get me. You know, when your thugs kidnapped me from your office, asshole."

Nydegger cringed at that knowing he was not over it…not really to his surprise. He focused, looking at the door, and seriously prayed that he would feel the warm sunshine on his face again, the sooner the better, he felt. Nydegger replied, "Like I said, Charlie, it ain't anything personal. I promise you, if I could be a million miles away from here, I happily would."

Charlie was nodding saying, "Yeah, I wish you were up in space. Like without a ship or a suit or air. Just floating there cold and dead."

Nydegger didn't say anything but picked up his phone dialing and advised when someone answered saying, "The boat needs repairs. I don't know if you have a secondary form of transportation for Mr. Ford or if you would simply like to extend the amount of time available with which he can have to achieve what he is supposed to be doing today. I cannot imagine that this is as easy as it sounds."

Charlie watched Nydegger nodding his head and was pretty sure he could tell that he wasn't going to tell anyone anything which they wanted to hear. Charlie was rolling his fingers trying to let Nydegger know that he should probably hurry the fuck up. These weren't the type of people you rushed and Nydegger smiled again showing no sincerity and no shortage of looking like he was gonna puke his guts out before saying,

"Well, I will relay that news to Mr. Ford. Thank you for letting me know that information."

Charlie asked, "Ask them how I get Jim and Tim back?"

Nydegger whispered back, "They will be dropped off after you do what has been asked of you."

Charlie replied, "So I'm supposed to trust the people that kidnapped my friends, broke into my boat, set up a fight in public and then want me to do something very illegal?"

Nydegger knew how stupid it sounded and couldn't say he blamed Charlie very much at all for having a lack of faith in the criminals. Nydegger said, "Yes, they would like you to please trust them."

Charlie tilted his head having issues believing a self-proclaimed lying lawyer and replied, "Tell you what, how about when I give them their shit they give me Jim and Tim. I'm sure anyone that's in charge of watching the two of them, especially Jim, are going to be dying to get rid of him."

Nydegger nodded, saying, "They said that that's fine and you can have two extra hours for boat repairs."

Charlie asked, "Wow, so generous. Is there anything else that I need to know?"

Nydegger relayed the question shaking his head no saying, "Other than the fact that if you don't do what they say that you'll be taken next, and the three of you will be tortured until you die. This is coming from them of course and they mentioned that they can make someone feel a very large amount of pain before finally dying. So please, please keep that in mind, won't you?"

Nydegger hung up the phone, sitting there for a moment, and Charlie stared him down advising, "This is when you should leave and be happy you can."

He absolutely did not need to be told twice. He got up, immediately reaching to grab the envelope, realizing it was supposed to stay with Charlie and then retracting his already mangled four finger hand.

Charlie watched, feeling no shortage of spite as he made his way out the boat door. He sat at his table seriously debating what the fuck he was going to do. Charlie knew his options couldn't be more limited at the moment, at least if he wanted to see his best friends in the world alive again. Unfortunately, Charlie was unsure if this was something that he would be able to do on his own but at the exact same time he didn't know if Johnney was going to be up for another round of absolute crazy or not. But, when resources were low sometimes you had to skim the bottom.

Charlie could not say he was overly excited about the prospect of doing anything illegal and would not be surprised if the moment…like the exact moment that he fulfilled his job that they would not happily or would happily put him down. He could see the three of them either being thrown in an unmarked grave out in the middle of nowhere or more than likely they would not even waste the time with doing such a thing and would just toss them into the waters on the open seas.

Chapter 8

Tim looked around as his eyes slowly allowed him to open them. It seemed like an understatement to say groggy at the moment. There was a wave of confusion that was hitting him first off. He had not been drugged before outside of maybe an appendix surgery which had been requested and some wisdom teeth. This definitely had faint memories of that. He couldn't actually tell at first what he was looking at. He didn't have contacts or glasses so this was a drug induced blur that he was dealing with at the moment. It took him a second, realizing what he was looking at was himself. His neck was hanging completely down and basically it was just a pair of gray cargo shorts and his very dark legs he was staring at.

Tim heard some murmuring going on and slowly started to lift his head completely up. He made it probably about three fourths of the way before his brain telling him what to do decided to take a nap on him. Tim's head fell back down, and he had to seriously force it to come back up again. When Tim thought that he had it figured out it started going down again when a warm palm caught him up against the forehead lifting his head up. He blinked the best that he could see, still trying to make sense of what the fuck was going on.

The finger in front of him was saying something and he didn't know if he didn't understand it or if it wasn't English that he was hearing. Whomever it was, was waving a flashlight back and forth in front of his vision and two fingers after the flashlight pressed into his neck which made him feel a bit thankful that he could feel his own pulse under the man's fingers. One thing his drill sergeant had said enough times that it could have been on a broken record was pain and a pulse would guarantee that you were still alive.

After the man was done with whatever he was doing, he let Tim's face go free and it bobbed as it bounced up and down still not having the motor skills to keep it under control. Tim was gaining at least his intelligence back thinking that if they were checking his vitals the chances were that they had not had any intentions of killing him. Tim started at the bottom working his way up thinking that getting his toes, then feet, etc. to wiggle would be the way to go. With his body size he knew that he'd hopefully get over it faster than if he were someone Charlie's size.

When his eyes were completely back to working order he tried to not make that a well-known fact. There wasn't a lot he could do at the moment, he knew, and when he heard a groaning, it was the same one that he had heard a million times before. Jim was not a pretty specimen when it came to dealing with hangovers. He was definitely a full-blooded Irishman, but when it came to the aftereffects, he didn't seem to understand that no matter how much or often he drank that there was no holding back when it came down to the nitty gritty facts that the night of question was King Kong…the day after he was the little monkey that hung out with Donkey Kong.

Tim had to try to not laugh when the pure misery his friend was feeling was being made out into a long groan. Jim asked, "What in the hell did I drink last night?"

Tim said, "Dude, shut up."

"I can't even open my eyes, how am I supposed to shut up?"

"By not talking; it is pretty simple."

"Can I ask one question?"

Tim knew keeping him quiet was one of the more impossible

tasks in life. It was actually an impossible task because to this day he at least hadn't ever achieved being able to do so. Tim said, "Just keep it down. I'm trying to keep those guys quiet. I don't want them to know that we are coming around."

"Okay, but did I eat sand last night, or did a cat mistake my mouth for a litter box and shit into it? Really, I'd like to know. I feel like maybe I should brush."

"Try getting up, stupid."

Jim looked through the same groggy eyes that Tim had and experienced the same results. There was not a lot that he could do to try and speed this process up which was less than ideal. Jim said, "So you might have started with telling me that we are tied up. How bad was I last night, or was it you?"

"Jim, I still don't have a clue what is happening. Someone came by, checked my pulse, and then left again. That's everything I can tell you right now other than I don't like this, and the guys were speaking Spanish, I am pretty sure."

"What did they say?"

"I don't know because I don't speak Spanish, which you probably already are well aware of this information. You know because we have known each other forever. So, if you've been paying attention then…"

"I thought you were the one telling me to shut up. Is there a reason that you don't think they can hear your voice? I'm sure that your voice is much deeper which would also lead me to believe that they would hear you before they hear me. What do you think about that?"

A voice in Spanish whispered something before a man in a somewhat broken English dialogue said, "We can hear you both, actually. The red one he snores, not a bueno one but ugly, very ugly. It pains me to listen to it."

Jim might have shut up had he been able to see everything going on in the facility, but much like Tim was still fucked up on the drugs, and that didn't seem to be the case at hand. Jim said, "Good news guys, I know Spanish."

Tim said, "No…no you don't, and you are going to say the wrong thing and get my ass shot or killed or god knows what."

Jim was coming around and said, "Mi gato está en llamas. Creo que orine mis pantalones cortos."

The two men stared at each other before the two of them broke out into a fit of laughter. The English-speaking man said, "What in the hell is he trying to say?"

Jim said, "Oh, I guess you aren't fluent in the language of love?"

Tim hissed from behind yelling, "That's French, you fucking idiot."

"Are you sure?"

"I'm sure as shit that it isn't Spanish, you dipshit. Now what in the hell do the two of you want? Why are we here, who are you?"

"Friends, amigo."

"My friends don't tie me up to chairs."

"Yes, well we probably aren't going to be great friends. But the good news is that your cat is not on fire, and I don't think you pissed yourself. You are going to be hanging out here for the day…hopefully, that is all."

Jim wasn't an idiot, and he didn't believe either of these guys. Unfortunately, he was trying to think of a way out of this. He was sure that Tim had been doing the same thing as soon as he had realized exactly what was going on here. It was not an ideal situation and he liked absolutely nothing about it. Jim said, "You wanna get out of here, Tim?"

"Please shut up. Yes, but just shut up please."

They both had their sight back about them now and were looking around, seeing that they were in some sort of warehouse. By the temperature there, they didn't believe in air conditioning. Jim said, "Wouldn't it be like the best if they just put us up in a hotel?"

Chapter 9

Charlie knew that he needed to get all of this shit figured out sooner than later. This did not sit well with him knowing that his friends were currently kidnapped and being held somewhere. He raced back up the dock seeing that Nydegger had already happily left and could not say that he was horribly surprised. He could only imagine the lawyer racing away like a bat out of hell. Johnney felt relieved, but only temporarily of course, when he saw Charlie coming back up the docks with no gun by his side this time. He could tell that Charlie still very much had the pistol as he could see the outline of it under his t-shirt. Johnney still had his gate in place and didn't look like he was getting ready to move it anytime soon for anyone. He asked, "Charlie, how goes it? Are you doing any of that detectiving yet?"

Charlie wasn't really sure how to answer that question. Charlie asked, "How busy are you right now, Johnney?"

Johnney wasn't an idiot in the least and asked right away, "Do you think that you could tell me what I would fill my time with? I mean if I wasn't busy and did have some free time?"

Charlie said, "You know I'm not gonna lie. This might actually be easier and safer than when you got recruited by Jim and Tim."

"Safer than having people chasing after me and trying to murder the four of us, oh do go on."

Charlie tried giving that winning smile, knowing the old man probably couldn't give a shit. Charlie said, "Yeah, you know it's no big deal. By the time you do this, I probably wouldn't need any help at all."

Johnney was nodding his head and Charlie was trying to figure out what he should do next. Charlie replied, "What I was kind of hoping, Johnney, was pretty easy. I'd like you to tear apart the engines on that boat. I'd like you to look really busy, but most importantly, I don't want you to change, fix, or break a single thing in there. All I need, please, is for you to buy me some time."

Johnney leaned in on his elbows, intrigued and curious and not to lie; a little worried about where this might all be going. Johnney questioned him saying, "And what am I supposed to do? I mean, you just want me to take some things off, look at it and put them back on. Hell, that won't take too long?"

"How long do you need?"

"I don't know, that's the problem, Johnney. But my thoughts are if you could just do what I asked I would definitely owe you one."

Johnney nodded his head saying, "Well, let me grab my toolbox. I can sit and pretend that I'm working for as long as you want. Just let me know when to put the shit back on the boat and we can call it good."

Charlie gave a thumbs up saying, "Well, perfect. If you get thirsty not working and trying to look like you're working, feel free to help yourself to all the beer in the fridge."

Johnney smiled saying, "Well you know what Jimmy says don't you? He says that it's always five o'clock somewhere in Margaritaville."

Johnney was already walking out with his tools asking, "What do you want me to do if anyone else shows up at the boat who shouldn't be there?"

Charlie said, "You take your shotgun down there. Put it somewhere where others might not see it, and if anything hits the fan I want you to use it."

"So, if my life is in danger then I should try and shoot them?"

"Yes…"

"Well, no shit, I was actually kidding. You think I need some kid to tell me to protect myself?"

Charlie at almost thirty never thought of himself as a kid but compared to Johnney figured so long as his acquaintances didn't lead to him getting killed that he had considerably more days left on Earth. Charlie really just hoped that if they figured out this day that he'd have a few more. Charlie had scribbled his number on a sheet of paper and was looking around the property doing his best to try and formulate some sort of a plan.

He'd also been thinking pretty hard about what he could do. The current circumstances meant he either needed to do one of two things, the first which was doing what these crooks or mobsters wanted him to do. This idea of course made him violently ill. The second idea which would make him feel a little better seemed like it was more up his alley. He'd never been really good about accepting threats or being intimidated. His uncle Joe had always mentioned that a balloon can be hit as hard as you want but it is always going to bounce back when you're done.

Charlie gave his watch a check on time, thinking he needed to get his ass in gear. He just didn't really have any ideas that he was capable of pondering at the moment that were going to get him set up. He was thinking about the last time and raced back to the boat hoping very much to find what he needed. Charlie did a search of both guy's rooms. The one or two things total that he was hoping to not find on the boat were both resting on Jim and Tim's nightstands. Cliff being at the right place at the right time had been the only reason that Charlie wasn't thirty feet plus under the ocean still today.

Charlie, not feeling any better after finding what he was looking for, walked back outside onto the deck. He hadn't had much time to process all the shit going on. Charlie looked up at the skies and as he gazed around not having anything to really look for he saw a red blinking light on a pole. Charlie focused on that for a minute seeing the black security camera. He felt like a light bulb had gone on and hoped his idea might lead him to a possible solution. Charlie looked at the other poles before realizing a fact he knew about rich people without question was that they liked to make sure that they kept their money and kept it safe. This of course, included the boats that they probably loved more than their spouses. At least that is what Charlie had noticed from his short time living down in the Keys. Charlie said, "Hey Johnney, how many cameras are there around here?"

"You were driving today right?"

"Yeah but I wasn't counting…"

"But you were using your eyes during all this time?"

Charlie was pretty sure he could tell what was coming his way and could not necessarily say he blamed the old man or was going to be overly surprised when he did say the next sentence. Charlie replied, "Yeah actually I was using my eyes believe it or not."

"Well good, then go ahead and use them just a little bit more and count. I don't have a fucking clue with all the cameras and shit and sticking all that info in clouds. I don't understand any of it and I hope I die before I have to, preferably though not because I've been helping you."

Again, Charlie definitely had not been surprised at that answer. Charlie was not the biggest fan of technology himself but was definitely beginning to think it was something he might want to look into. The modern-day detective just might need to know a thing or two about a thing or two, he thought. Charlie replied, "Thanks for all that help, Johnney. I really appreciate it."

Johnney gave a thumbs up as he walked down to the boat saying, "Hey, anytime. See, us old guys gotta make sure you young bucks got some fucking common sense. We can't have you getting old and going out asking dumbass questions all the time."

"Well, you're a gent and a scholar, Johnney."

Johnney who obviously had zero worries about anyone hearing what he said or how he said it yelled, "Well a gent and a scholar I am fucking am not, but I also don't say anything unless it's gonna add something to the world: no dumbass questions for me. And hey, if it's something I can do all on my own without asking then I do that too."

Charlie smiled not necessarily wanting to give a guy that was definitely helping him out the finger even though he thought it would feel quite satisfying. Charlie gave a thumbs up walking saying, "Well I'm just gonna go count and use my eyes. I mean if that's okay with you?"

Johnney started taking the heads off of the covers of the engines yelling, "Just call me when you need me to be done not working."

Charlie gave him a thumbs up again, hoping that he wasn't going to need the boat to go and do what was supposed to be done. The only way he wanted to go to those coordinates is if he was locked and loaded and ready to cut those fucks down. Charlie asked, "What's your number?"

"What number?"

"The number to call you?"

"Well, I thought you'd call the shack line."

"How are you gonna hear that?"

"At this age, I'm not going to, Jesus, I thought you were the smart one?"

"I'll just come back to the dock, how's that sound? Hopefully, I don't have anyone coming this way with guns a blazing."

Johnney held up his shotgun saying, "Well, we are going to be able to give you a little time."

Charlie gave a thumbs up. There wasn't a whole helluva lot more that needed to be said. By the time Charlie had made his way to the truck, he had realized very quickly he wasn't alone. Charlie was not opposed to company, but he was quite confident that this one was not here to do anything but follow him. Charlie had definitely had his share of experience having to watch people and see what they did to make sure that they needed to be taken care of. But his was in a criminal justice circumstance scenario. So, the first thing he did was heading out quickly and turning and giving it just a little gas.

The man was obviously trying to be inconspicuous in a blacked out black Escalade. Charlie could only question if these people all seem to get discounts from the Cadillac company. He wondered if he did enough jobs if maybe he could get a detective's version, preferably with built in cameras all around. He knew at some point he would be hired to get evidence on a cheating spouse. It would be ideal to have proof of who damaged the vehicle so he could get reimbursed to have the vehicle fixed.

Charlie took a left going down Spielman Street. Still keeping an eye and noticing the Cadillac that would have stayed multiple cars back had there been room for that to happen. Charlie took a few more turns; if this guy was a professional, he was pretty shitty at his job, or maybe he just hadn't done it before. Everyone thought the tasks that policemen do were simple, until they actually were required to try and do them. After two more normal turns of Charlie not really laying on the gas he took one more and punched the accelerator, taking off like a bat out of hell.

Chapter 10

As soon as Charlie was up to going twenty over he saw that the guy tailing him was doing an even worse job than he had thought he was. The Escalade guy was seriously racing to get up on Charlie's ass. He wasn't doing great and with no other cars there weren't really many places for him to hide. Charlie assumed that unlike himself who had been trained in defensive driving that this guy didn't know the first thing.

Charlie knew about ten different ways he could probably crash into this guy and keep his truck, maybe not looking amazing but definitely useful. Unfortunately, this being their only vehicle at the moment made that option a shitty one. Charlie raced down zig zagging through the streets turning three times and feeling like he'd used his free time wisely spending it driving around and memorizing the city. Charlie figured there'd be plenty of stakeouts so it would probably be intelligent to know his way about. Charlie knew that no one was going to be out to kill him, or they probably would have just waited for him to arrive back at the boat. No, this was merely people making sure he was doing what they said he should be doing.

Charlie was trying to think of anything he could to get this guy off his ass and keep it that way. He knew if he made his next phone call and already had trouble behind him that he would undoubtedly get a go fuck yourself answer when he requested the help. Not that he would like the answer but wouldn't be real happy or be able to blame said person for when it came down to answering.

Charlie saw what looked like a pretty empty gas station. Charlie turned last minute into the driveway, taking the back tires over the curb. The truck was going too fast for this, and he had to slam on the brakes or risk driving straight into the pumps. He knew this wasn't the movies, but he was imagining crashing into them going full speed and dying in a horrific fiery blaze. Charlie looked around the parking lot. There were only two cars there and from what he could only assume was that one belonged to the gas station clerk. The other, he figured, was some friend sitting there shooting the shit while he was probably supposed to be working. Charlie slid to a stop next to the pumps. The gas station had two entrances and Charlie wasted no time choosing quickly which one he would be leaving through. He could tell that the two in the store were giving him their full attention. Charlie smiled nervously as these guys were in for a show.

Charlie had his truck door open and smiled, waving as the man pulled to a quick stop barking the tires on the Escalade and opened his door to get out. Charlie held up a finger as he was finishing lighting one of his uncle's expensive cigars. He hadn't really had the heart yet to clean out most of Uncle Joe's things in there. Right now, though, a cigar that would stay lit was his best friend. Charlie waited to see if the guy was going to listen or not, apparently not was the answer. Charlie very happily shrugged and inhaled as hard as he could. Charlie made the cigar glow as he took a giant puff and made it burn a crimson red like in the fire of night. Charlie flicked the cigar and it seemed pretty goddamn quick that the Escalade guy figured out that maybe it would be in his best interest to get his ass back into the SUV.

Charlie didn't even look over his shoulder; he simply got back into the truck and put it in gear. Finally looking in his rear view seeing that a fireball of hell was taking place and growing larger by the second. The guy in the Escalade immediately disappeared because the flames had become higher than his SUV. Charlie had soaked the driveway including the entrance pretty sure that this guy would choose backing up over burning in an inferno.

Charlie couldn't have been more right. When he backed up Charlie pulled out with a very irate gas station attendee who was waving his middle fingers in the air, violently. He did feel a little guilty about it, but he didn't feel bad enough to put his life on the line. He'd at least made sure to shoot the gas far enough away from the pumps to not blow them up. He wasn't an arsonist and hadn't really planned on becoming one. When he got some distance between them Charlie slowed down the truck to only going twenty over. He didn't want to run some kid over just because he didn't think that it was a good time to have a tail.

Chapter 11

Cliff was sitting at his apartment. His girlfriend had made it extremely painfully and unquestionably clear that if Cliff did not find a new job very goddamn soon that the only thing he'd be entering in their apartment would be doorways. Cliff very much did not think being celibate sounded enjoyable whatsoever and had promised her that he would do anything he could once he figured something out. Of course, Cliff had absolutely no idea what that thing was going to be. But did know that eventually her paychecks were not going to be enough and what little amount they had saved would just keep dwindling away until it was as if they had never actually had any savings to begin with.

Cliff was looking online already extremely confident that he had zero interest in chauffeuring anyone anytime soon. Unless it was for like a large corporation because more than likely he wouldn't have to worry about thugs and mobsters and dirty lawyers…well, maybe the dirty lawyers, but he could handle that if it didn't mean he needed to see a gun on a daily basis. He also did not want to have to tell his girlfriend again that he almost died on the job and in all actuality had not even gotten paid for it.

He knew that Nydegger owed him some money but that was the last office that he ever wanted to go into again. Cliff was thinking how cool it had been minus being shot at to get to actually use a little bit of his techie skills. He would have loved to be able to find a job where doing something like that could maybe be a regular thing. Cliff knew not everyone was able to do such things so maybe if he kept looking and probably praying a little bit that he might, just might, find a job doing such a thing.

Cliff looked at his iPhone on the coffee table. It was dancing around and blinking. He peered at it trying to see if it was his girlfriend, but it wasn't and the one thing he hated most about job searches was having to answer numbers that he didn't know. The last thing he hoped to do was let his girlfriend Chandra know that he had missed a call from someone who might have a job to offer and not really have any good reason other than probably pure laziness why he had missed the call. A loving woman she was but a forgiving woman she was not and a pissed off woman she sure as shit could be. Cliff lunged for it, hitting the answer button saying, "Hello."

Charlie was so nervous about having to get so many things

figured out so quickly that he kind of just acted like when he called Cliff it was a call that he might make when he was calling Jim or Tim. Charlie said, "Hi Cliff, is this a good time?"

Charlie didn't necessarily care if his answer was no. This was definitely what someone might refer to as a time sensitive task. Cliff was trying to be as professional as possible and said, "This is Cliff thank you. If you don't mind, can I ask which human resources company you're with?"

Charlie had kind of not thought about the fact that Cliff having a code of ethics and not enjoying getting shot at had probably left him unemployed. He knew that wasn't necessarily all his fault but nonetheless it didn't make him feel one damn bit better. Charlie responded really hoping that he didn't just hang up saying, "Well, I actually am not calling for any companies…"

Those words hit him like a brick. Cliff cut him off saying, "Hey I don't mean to be an asshole man but if you're calling to sell me shit I ain't got shit. I'm in between jobs, at some point I'll probably have one and maybe I'll even listen to your spiel. But today ain't that day. I need to find a job before my woman kicks me out on my ass, if you know what I mean."

Charlie said, "I'm not trying to sell you anything, Cliff. This is Charlie Ford, you know, from the boat."

Cliff had an immediate flashback of everything that had happened that night. He couldn't say that he was dying to relive that experience all over again. He had his finger hovering over the end button but figured if he hadn't heard from this guy in a month that chances were probably strong that if Charlie was calling it was because help was needed. That wasn't necessarily something Cliff was dying to do but also didn't want to leave anyone in a shitty situation if he could help it. Cliff responded, trying not to sound like he was going to be excited to help or even really entertain the thought, "Yeah I remember you. You could say that your issues had somewhat of an impact on my life."

"I can't pay you a ton. But do you think you might be able to help me out with something? I'm hoping that you're as good with techy shit as you were on the night I was taken."

Cliff perked up a little, thinking. So long as no one knew who it was that he could probably handle whatever he needed to have done. He liked computers. You could be a far distance away from people and not get shot at. Those were a few of the things that were probably his favorite in life. Cliff said, "Yeah, I'm pretty good with the tech stuff. That was definitely something that I enjoyed getting to do that night. I wasn't the biggest fan of bullets coming my way regardless of where I was in the boat."

Charlie replied, "Well I'm really, really hoping that no one is going to get shot at."

"Funny how you say that, because it makes it sound like it's not actually one of those guaranteed things in life. It sounds more like yeah, there's a chance that we might have some issues. That isn't necessarily really what I was going for. Could you tell me maybe a little about what I need to do?"

"Yeah, I need you to help me trace a boat. I want to know where it ended up going and I would like to be as discreet about it as possible. Is that something that you think you might be able to handle?"

"You do realize that I'm not a professional right?"

Charlie smiled saying, "Great, that means I can pay you less."

"Well, quite frankly considering my current wage I would have to say that it would be better than nothing. I know you'd probably find this hard to believe but Nydegger is not big on paying for unemployment. He is kind of a real son of a bitch. Kind of fits everything you think about scumbag lawyers."

Charlie said, "I tell you what, how about I give you 300 bucks for one day's work. I'm not rich either, but I would like to be one day. I'm not quite sure how the hell that would happen but, by God, I would not look a gift horse in the mouth if the option was there and preferably legal."

Cliff thought that 300 for a day's work was damn good, especially since he didn't think that Charlie would be handing him over any forms to file taxes. Cliff, who wasn't a sucker or stupid, asked, "Two quick questions."

"Shoot."

"Well yeah that's kind of one of them. Will I be shot at?"

"No, you should not be shot at."

"Question one, awesome answer. Number two, can I expect that you're going to pay me in cash and not a check?"

"Yeah, it'll be cash, and you might even get a bonus."

Cliff liked the idea of a bonus. He liked the idea of cash. He liked the idea of being able to tell Chandra that he was going to get some money. Cliff figured so long as he wasn't up to any illegal shit, which he never was, that Chandra would be more than content. The only thing Cliff didn't like was that he still didn't actually know what the job was. Cliff asked, "What am I doing? Is it anything illegal?"

"Well, I don't think so."

"You don't think it's illegal?"

"Yeah, I mean I doubt it is, fifty-fifty."

"You're definitely filling me with a lot of confidence, Charlie. Are the other two guys gonna be with us? You know the ones that dead lifted and carried me on to the fucking boat where I was shot at?"

"Actually, that's kind of the job."

Cliff wasn't understanding any of it because he was being a little bit more vague than he liked to be and Cliff said, "You want me to get paid to be dead lifted by your friends?"

"Close, I need you to find my friends."

"I thought you guys were going to be detectives? I saw Jim with a bullet hole through his shoulder talking to that reporter. Did you guys decide not to do that?"

"No, that's exactly what I still want to do. But they are currently missing and the only idea that I have to be able to try and find them is involving technology which I don't currently at least understand how to do what would need to be done."

"Well, it sounds like you probably should learn how to do some of that shit."

Charlie said, "Do you have a laptop or computer?"

"Really? You think I'm gonna take this job and then try to do everything from my cell phone?"

"Cliff..."

"Yes, yes I've got a fucking computer. I've got a laptop too. They're both awesome. I could tell you about them, but it sounds like it probably wouldn't make much difference."

"You would be correct."

"Do you want me to come to your place? Otherwise, we can meet somewhere so long as you don't mind having these conversations out loud."

"I'll meet you at a coffee shop. How's that sound?"

"Sure, how about Leslie's Diner?"

"No offense to Leslie's place. But that place is stupidly packed this time of year and I also need Wi-Fi. I don't have that package on my phone, and they are still in the stone age."

"No worries, I don't either. Probably wouldn't be a stupid thing to get though, for me anyways. Just text me where you want to meet me, and I'll be there as soon as I can. This job is somewhat on a tricky and time sensitive schedule. So, the quicker that we can get this completed would probably be for the better."

"Yeah, I'll be quick. I just need five or ten minutes to get my bag put together with all my nerdy shit and I'll hit the road."

Chapter 12

Jim and Tim were still tied to their metal chairs facing back-to-back. It was not ideal given the fact that neither man obviously wanted to be there. Unfortunately, though for Tim, Jim was not as usual taking his advice. Tim had told him to just keep the guys away from them and that they could ride this through until whatever needed done was done. They both figured it had to do something with Charlie because other than him, Fratto, and a crooked detective and maybe a lawyer they really didn't know anyone all that well that would constitute having to get kidnapped over.

Jim who always had something to say cleared his throat saying, "Waiter Waiter? Table service please. I need a little help."

The trio of men watching the two of them to make sure they stayed put looked over after a few minutes of Jim being obnoxious. One of them walked over asking, "What the fuck do you want?"

"I wanted to see the dinner menu. If you have any specials, that would be great to hear. If it wouldn't put you out too much could we get the wine list?. I'm thinking maybe something from the red family. Do you know if duck is on the menu today? We are celebrating something special. This is our first time getting kidnapped."

The man pulled out a knife pushing one button that brought a blade out the front. He waved it in front of Jim's eyes smiling and saying, "How about tongue? Would tongue on the menu be good for you, bitch?"

Jim closed his lips shaking his head no and when the man put the knife away and turned around he said, "Waiter, I'm sorry to do this again. But I must ask, would I be able to change the bandages on my shoulder?"

He looked at Jim not really hesitating much before saying, "Yeah, sure. Good luck with that."

Jim said, "Well I was actually thinking that maybe you could untie me so I could do that."

The man or aka Jim's make-believe waiter who Tim was pretty sure would be getting pissed much sooner than later said, "I highly doubt that."

"You doubt letting me go? Or that I can change my own bandage? If you're gentle I could let you do it. But you'd have to wash your hands first. No offense, but infections are no laughing matter."

"No, I doubt that you were thinking. You seem like a very stupid man, one that does not make wise decisions. I would be surprised if this is your first time in a situation like this."

Tim said, "You should really shut the fuck up, Jim. Anything that happens to you is probably going to come my way too, and I don't think that that's fair."

"Would I ever do anything to hurt you, intentionally?"

"Unintentionally still hurts, Jim. That's my concern."

"All I'm saying, Tim, is in the end it might be better for you."

The man didn't seem like he was overly concerned about Jim's wound or need to urinate. He did pull the shirt down, taking a look at the bandaged shoulder pulling it down all the way and seeing that it had gone where he could assume from the very light faint hint of blood on both sides which was always better than having a bullet be shaken around like a tic tac inside of your body. Even the smallest bullet could cause a hell of a lot of damage. He said, "Shit, I've seen much worse than this. You should be happy for the care that you've gotten. At least someone knew what they were doing."

"Yes, I always feel thankful after being shot in the arm with a gun."

The man patted Jim directly on the wound, "Yes we have smart asses like you where I come from as well. Do not worry, if things don't go well, I will teach you a few things about pain before I let you die."

Jim smiled, saying, "You're just too good to us. You're too good to be true."

The man walked around looking at Tim directly asking, "I bet he gets you in some pretty serious shit, doesn't he?"

Tim kinda just let his body relax and the deflated hopeless look was more than enough to answer the man. Their phones all began to ring at once, and without hesitation, they raced out of the room.

*****

Tim brought his head forward just a little and back quite a bit harder, popping Jim in the back of the head. Tim forgot, Jim had just as hard of a head as he did. Jim said, "I don't think they like me. I don't think they like us; I mean?"

"No, they don't like you. I however am the perfect hostage. Now shut up, don't talk to anyone. Don't ask for anything. All of those attributes make a good hostage."

"Well, what if we decided we didn't want to be hostages anymore?"

"Well, I would think that would probably be a fantastic idea. Now could you possibly tell me how in the hell such a thing could possibly happen? I mean, I think the entire time we haven't wanted to be hostages but being here and tied up has not made that easy for anyone."

"Well see, the first thing we need to do is get the handcuffs off. Then the next thing we're going to do is to get the zip ties off and then when they come back in what I would really like to do is take that knife that he threatened to cut my poetic tongue out with, and I'd like to stab it into his jugular. Then I'm taking his pistol and shooting the other two, point blank in the foreheads."

Tim could never understand the optimism his ugly Irishman friend seemed to come up with in a moment's notice. He replied, "So that all sounds great. But exactly how in the hell do you expect to do a portion of that, or hell, any of that?"

"Oh, so this is all on me to figure out, the wounded best friend. You know if Charlie was here he probably wouldn't be nearly as optimistic as me."

"Charlie would have been trying to get out of this stuff the entire time."

"You know, Tim, I do have feelings."

"Yes, I'm aware. I have a feeling right now that if you don't shut up those guys are gonna start cutting pieces of you off. Is that what you want to have happen?"

"No, I quite like the idea of them staying out of here for like ten minutes so I can get us out of this."

Tim almost never took anything he said seriously but, if this was actually a possibility then he could not say he was not 110 percent on board. He couldn't help himself but ask, "Are you serious or are you just fucking with me?"

Tim could hear little movements, grunts, and curses from Jim sitting behind him and was definitely trying to figure out what the hell he was doing. Jim said, "Now Tim, you need to be quiet because I'm trying to focus. Do you understand what focusing means, Tim?"

"You realize if you aren't actually getting us out, I'm going to kill you, right? I mean, you know, if the Colombian thugs don't end up doing it first."

"You know how you guys say I waste too much time on YouTube? Well, fortunately for you there's actually a hell of a lot of useful stuff on there. I figured with all that free time it might not be the stupidest thing to keep a few tricks of the trade on me at all times. I'd have to guess these guys don't frequent YouTube for hours on end learning vital and important stuff like I have."

Tim tried to turn around in his seat a little bit to see what the hell he was talking about but that wasn't actually possible. Jim pulled a small strip of metal from under his belt loop. After he'd found the video and gotten it once he'd watched quite a few more videos and picked up some helpful tips for how to hide some stuff on your person.

Jim cursed after he dropped the first piece of metal that was so thin and so light neither of them could hear it as it bounced off of the chair down onto the ground. It put it at an unreachable distance below. Jim said, "Whoops."

"Whoops, what do you mean whoops? What are you doing? What did you drop?"

"Dude it's okay. Just relax. Try those breathing exercises."

"Breathing is probably one of my top priorities right now, Jim. So please for the love of God tell me what you're doing. Is there anything I can do to help?"

"You mean besides shutting up?"

"Okay, okay, fine just do it."

Jim had to stretch in a weird angle to be able to get the next piece of metal. He slid it where the rivets for the handcuffs would click with each notch as they tightened. Lucky for Jim these guys thought having the zip ties and the handcuffs would be more than enough. Tim, not knowing, was driving him ape shit. He could hear the click as the cuff was getting tighter wondering what the hell he was doing until the clicking noise stopped and the sound of the cuff freeing itself and clattering against the seat became audible.

Jim knew the zip ties were next; he also knew this was going to leave a mark. He pried against the ties until they finally broke free. Jim was feeling like a soon to be free man at the moment. The duct tape that they had wrapped them to the metal folding chairs was all that was left. Tim said, "Christ did you snap those off?"

"Yeah, gimme a second to get this tape off. I learned this one on Rachael Ray."

Tim wanted to say something about his manhood but just as

soon as Jim had quit talking he leaned back and then forward tearing the tape almost effortlessly all at once. He had never been so happy for someone to have useless information in his entire life.

Jim walked around smiling. Tim didn't think that the look Jim was giving could be summarized so simply by saying he was being smug. He didn't know if even the dictionary would have such a word. But the amount of pride Jim was currently and as annoying as it was completely deservingly showing would have been enough to make him laugh any other time. Jim sat on Tim's lap saying, "So, just between the two of us, are you going to be able to live with yourself if I free you?"

"It'll take time. But it'll be the better alternative to if you don't free me in the next few minutes and we live through this I will fucking kill you. I'm not in a joking manner. So, please, pretty please, I could not mean this more. Get me out of these cuffs please."

Jim tapped him on the nose saying, "You know what, buttercup? I think I believe you. That sounded just about as sincere as you could imagine."

Jim slid the piece of metal trying to tighten it, but they had already apparently been worried about Tim being able to break free of them and there quite literally was no way possible to make the cuffs any tighter. Which also made it impossible to be able to get the piece of metal under the cuff to make it break loose and slide free. Tim said, "You do realize they're going to come back right? The bad guys always come back."

"Yeah but there's like only three of them."

"Yeah D-bag. There's three of them with guns and at least one with a knife and all three don't like you."

"That hurts my feelings. I thought only two of them didn't like me. Maybe just one. It's hard to tell sometimes with those strong macho Colombian types."

"Look around for something that you can get the fucking cuffs broken open with would you?"

Jim scoured the area looking around before saying, "You know, funny enough, there's no bolt cutters or anything in this factory. I actually don't even know what in the hell they do here. Maybe this is just where they do illegal shit."

The door began to open, and Jim knew if they saw he was loose that they would probably try and shoot him first and take care of Tim just so that there wasn't any liability. He raced over, sitting down hoping they wouldn't notice the broken duct tape that was still plastered to his front. The guy walked over looking at the two of them. Jim had a smile as wide as could be. He waited, looking over his shoulder, still smiling. Still waiting and watching until the two men out of the three had taken their seats at the small card table and began dealing a deck of cards. Jim whispered, "Hey, waiter, guess what, your guys are looking at the cards. They're totally fucking you."

The man snapped his head back towards the two men. He apparently was not a large fan of people cheating and screamed, "You bitches better not be fucking with my cards. I'll fucking kill you if you are cheating!"

Jim said, "Now that's not very nice, Mr. Waiter."

When he turned around thinking it'd be nice to cut this guy's tongue out Jim was already standing. The maître d' as Jim had expected immediately began reaching for his pocket to either pull out a pistol or a knife. Jim didn't know and didn't care mostly because he wasn't going to have the opportunity to do what he wanted to do with them regardless of his weapon of choice. Jim used the only thing that was going to be useful on him. He had closed both sets of cuffs again, making them small and a makeshift pair of brass knuckles.

Jim was no slouch when it came to punching. The night he was shot if it would have been his dominant right arm, the guy still would have to worry about Jim being able to seriously fuck someone up with his left. He swung as hard as he possibly could, connecting hard and directly into the man's somewhat gold grill. The sound of the cuffs on his teeth and lips was actually not loud at all. But the number of teeth that began dribbling out of his mouth along with what seemed like a never-ending flow of blood was absolutely and unquestionably disgusting. His lips became drenched in crimson pouring down his face and neck and drenching his shirt.

Chapter 13

Charlie drove like a bat out of hell to a Starbucks where he thought their coffee tasted like assholes but agreed the yuppie assholes would have Wi-Fi. Cliff already had a laptop set up and motioned for him to swing over. Cliff stood when Charlie came up to the table. The two shook hands getting pleasantries out of the way and Charlie said, "Are you ready to work?"

"Yeah, so long as you're really going to pay cash, Charlie."

Charlie pulled out a folded wad and dropped three one-hundred-dollar bills to show that he was definitely good for it. Cliff looked around and Charlie said, "Don't worry, folks, it's not a drug deal. Well, not a big one at least."

That statement made none of the baristas or customers feel a single bit better. Charlie sat down and laid it out for him, "So, here's what I need. Tim and Jim apparently are spending some time against their will somewhere else."

Charlie was going to continue but Cliff said, "You're sure about this? Also, are you sure that this is legal?"

"Well, it's probably legal-ish. I mean, maybe just don't get caught doing it."

"You know who says that…people doing illegal shit. That statement makes me feel a hell of a lot better. But how do you know that they were taken? They're grown ass men. Couldn't they have just gone somewhere?"

Charlie dropped the picture of the boys down in front of Cliff and said, "Long story short, I went to a diner. Mystery envelopes showed up, that picture of Jim and Tim with guns to their head and sleeping was in it. It makes me think they were drugged, and I actually feel kind of bad for the poor bastard that had to carry them. Tim is a big motherfucker. My scumbag lawyer, your previous employer, was waiting for me when I arrived and basically laid out what I needed to do. He gave me GPS coordinates and told me that I needed to be there within twelve hours."

"So, what, you need me to look up the coordinates? I mean I can but Jesus for three hundred bucks you probably could have just done a Google search for free. Not looking a gift horse in the mouth, trust me."

"Well, that's good because I'm not asking you to look up GPS coordinates. That's definitely something I know how to do. What I do need from you, is to hack into a computer system for me or possibly multiple computer systems and tell me where in the hell my friends are."

"Uh huh, and how exactly am I supposed to get into these systems? And do you even know which systems I am supposed to get into?"

Charlie realized he didn't know any of this shit and chances were damn strong that Cliff was going to have to earn that three hundred. Charlie replied, "First, I need you to get into the cameras at the docks. I can't imagine that place is too high tech. However, after that I don't have a clue. I figured if the boat went right or left we would look up to see what place there is…and then we, or by we I mean you, hack into the next computer, and so on."

"And what are you wanting with all this info?"

"Damn it, you're a smart one. I figured you'd know this. That one's easy. What I want is for you to hack enough different cameras that I'm able to figure out where they took my friends."

"So that you can call the police?"

Charlie shrugged saying, "Call the police, go there, and rescue them. Go there and rescue and shoot the bad guys in the head. Then maybe go back to Nydegger and shoot him as well just for good measure so he never comes into my life again."

Cliff smiled and said, "Hey, not to freak you out or anything, I mean further freak you out. But there's some guys outside that look like they are watching you."

Charlie looked at his phone with the selfie mode on and checked behind him to see that it was Detective Lindvall. That was not ideal at the moment. When he moved it a little bit more he noticed that Raul was there as well. Luckily, they did not seem to know each other. This was absolutely okay by Charlie. He replied, "Fuck, that's just great. It's probably best if I bounce and you figure out this info without having to worry about the two D-bags outside coming in."

"Boy this sure kind of feels familiar you know; compared to

the last time I worked with you guys you know against my will."

"Hey, just think of all the great job skills you're getting. You're going to be super employable for anyone that's in need of any kind of work such as this."

"Yeah I can only imagine how much fun it would be having this as a daily thing to worry about."

"Well, at least you'll always have in-demand skills. Hit me up as soon as you figure something out, will you?"

Charlie got up to head out before Lindvall could head in. Lindvall stopped dead in his tracks when Charlie walked out the door. The two of them weren't really the type to pretend they liked people when they didn't. So, neither did. Charlie was going to walk right past him, but Lindvall held up a hand saying, "You're not doing any jobs are you, Charlie?"

"No, I haven't taken any paying clients on as of yet."

"No work in the Keys, hmm?"

"No, that's actually not it at all. See, whatever complete and utter ass wipe dickhead piece of shit that's in charge of approving them for some reason hasn't. I couldn't imagine why an ex-navy man couldn't get approved."

Lindvall could feel his stomach growing warm and had to try and settle himself down just a hair. He said, "Well that's not a very nice way to talk about the people who protect this great community is it?"

"Well, I guess if the shoe fits. I mean, I'm all for having police protection taking care of the city answering calls. You know, but when it comes down to people doing illegal shit on the city's dime and then at the same time they also think that maybe they should make additional money on the side working for criminals. Then to make the matters so much worse they don't want to do anything to help someone who's actually going to provide a valuable service and something to the city with a business proposition."

Lindvall said, "Well geez I guess you'll just have to wait and pray, won't you, Charlie?"

"Yep, I guess so. I'm headed out, you headed in to get a coffee,

Lindvall?"

"It's detective Lindvall, thanks."

"I said as much as I wanted to. Don't worry, there's ten or fifteen other names I would have rather called you. I'd be happy to list them off for you, alphabetically if you like?"

"Oh really? Did you want to try any of those out and see how they fit?"

"No, busy day and all I don't have time to go to jail. Because then I'd have to sit there and wait and break out again or have a lawyer come and get me. You know I can always call my lawyer if you want to. I'm sure a harassment case against the Keys Police Department would just absolutely make his day. I'm pretty sure that the retainer is covered for the foreseeable future for him. He seemed like a lovely man."

Lindvall remembered how easily he'd gotten them out. Of course, he hadn't actually had any reason to take them to jail in the first place. He replied, "No, I wouldn't want to keep you from whatever important things you have going on today, Charlie."

"Well, why don't you go ahead and enjoy your coffee and maybe skip the donut, Lindvall. You're not looking real trim around the middle, if you know what I mean."

"Yeah, go fuck yourself, Ford."

"And a good fucking I will have thank you so much," Charlie said as he walked away both men shaking their heads in disgust of the other. Charlie headed towards his truck waiting for Lindvall to get inside and turned around smiling and walked up to Raul saying, "Is there a reason that you're following me now?"

"I saw your truck on my way to the gym. I thought that maybe you and I should actually meet face to face."

"Well, it'd be great if you leave my other four fucking tires alone because the spare's on it and I haven't had time to go get a patch job done."

"You think that I would need to stab your tire to take you out?"

"No, not to take me out. I just figured you were being a

dickhead. I mean would that be a fair assessment?"

Raul shrugged leaning against his car that Charlie was quite sure was obnoxiously loud with a muffler and probably a system to boot. He had the dickhead warning sign with a giant spoiler on a car with a four cylinder in it.

Charlie said, "See, I didn't think you were here for me anyway. I thought you were here for that guy that just went into the coffee shop. You know Candace's new boyfriend? She must have wanted the complete opposite after you because man he's a fat fuck compared to your skinny ass."

Raul went from a somewhat intimidating pissed off looking guy but that very quickly morphed into a jealous rage fit. Raul pointed to Lindvall who was getting a coffee and something to eat saying, "My Candace does not date that man? You know why because that man is dead!"

Charlie said, "I'm only telling you what I know. It's not like I'm a matchmaker, shit, the details could be completely wrong that I heard. I mean if you were a little nicer to her she might still be around but I'm pretty sure that you know you've kind of fucked that up beyond all things fixable."

"Oh really?"

Charlie shrugged, "Well yeah, he was just saying that he saw you over there and quite frankly doesn't see why everyone thinks you're so tough. I think he said you kind of look like a pussy."

"That pussy called me a pussy?"

"Yeah, sometimes he talks too fast though. It might have been something about your mom too. I don't know or your sister. I know he needs to slow down when he talks is what I'm getting at."

"He's fucking dead. Get the fuck out of my way."

"Raul, I hope you have the most pleasant day."

Charlie got in his truck thinking hey at the very least Raul might get thrown in jail for a little bit and might buy him a little time to figure out what to actually do with the prick. Charlie turned the truck over, not hating that air conditioning when it kicked on. He watched a very pissed off and motivated Raul walking with a purpose directly across the street. He didn't stop when cars were honking their horns for him to get out of the street.

Raul pushed the door open without hesitation. He placed one hand on Lindvall's shoulder and spun him around. Lindvall, who apparently had purchased a cookie and was currently trying to eat said cookie, looked as surprised as anyone; mostly because he had zero clues why in the hell this tiny muscular tattooed man was coming up to him looking like he was in an absolute fit of rage.

Charlie would feel bad for both of these guys…if they were good people. However, in his personal, somewhat biased opinion he thought they were complete fucking assholes. He wasn't quite sure what Raul was gonna do, but short of him pulling out a pistol and trying to shoot Lindvall, he figured that he'd still be able to sleep at night.

Lindvall looked over his shoulder trying to see if he had bought the last cookie because he didn't know what in the hell this guy was so infuriated about. Lindvall had decided after looking that it didn't actually matter because it looked like a punch was coming his way regardless. Lindvall tried to set down his cookie when Raul punched him square in the face three times as hard as he possibly could. Charlie could see the new shape of Lindvall's nose and was pretty sure he had just had his shit broken. Between Raul probably going to jail and Lindvall needing to go get his nose work done probably sooner than later he hoped it would buy him the few hours needed to get the things done that he needed to. The only thing in his master plan he might not have considered was the fact that he had just unleashed all that shit right where Cliff was trying to do the work that he was paying him for so he could find and hopefully rescue his friends.

Lindvall put his hands up to his nose. This didn't stop Raul though; he simply began punching him in the gut, turning Lindvall around and punching him in the kidneys, treating this like nothing short of a street fight...the type taking place in a commercial yuppie coffee franchise shop. Lindvall used his considerably girthier amount of weight to push himself backwards slamming Raul's lean frame into the glass door that did not budge in the direction he needed it to. Raul let out an oomph when he hit the glass.

When Lindvall turned around for all the shortcomings Raul might have had in the intelligence department, one sure fire thing he did know how to notice was a police-issued Glock with a badge plastered on the front of his pants clipped to his belt. Raul used his feet to try and kick Lindvall away and it worked quite effectively. Raul put his hands on the bar of the door, bringing up his knees and kicking his legs out, catching him in the gut. Raul wanted to get out of there before he ended up in handcuffs. The list of charges was already racing through his head. Charlie couldn't lie, he was glad the truck was on because if Raul decided that he needed to now come after Charlie, he thought until he had a better handle on the situation that he might just drive away. He wasn't afraid to bleed but also knew when he was potentially outmatched which felt like this might be that case.

Raul got the door open and seemed like someone hit pause on his remote. His face was filled with rage which turned into a horrific expression of pain. This was pain that he didn't know if Raul had probably ever felt in his life. Charlie was pretty sure he knew what was going down and when Raul continued not moving, blinking, or changing his cheeks or lips in any way, Charlie was pretty sure he was getting tasered. Lindvall took Raul by the neck after he let off the juice flowing into him. He took him by the rear of the neck, slamming him face first into the glass.

Lindvall didn't give a shit if this guy lived or died right now. He had just absolutely ruined what small joy he thought he was going to have today with his coffee and cookie. He knew damn well if there hadn't been this many bystanders and he had this broken nose that he would happily just put one in the back of his head once he had staged it correctly. Lindvall knew he had a carry piece that was the perfect ditch gun to say was someone else's.

Lindvall hit the electricity one more time and let off the volts while walking. He lifted Raul by the back of the neck and threw him down to the ground. Lindvall didn't let up and placed a knee in the middle of his back as he fished for a pair of handcuffs. Charlie could tell that he was not leaving any room for circulation. Charlie drove off, stopping a half a block up. He watched Lindvall holding a handful of napkins up to his nose, not looking like he was feeling amazing at the moment.

He manhandled Raul until he got back to his unmarked car. Lindvall opened the door, slamming Raul's face into it as he opened the rear up. Lindvall took Raul by the rear of his pants and neck, lifting him up effortlessly, throwing him violently into the door on the opposite side.

Lindvall slammed the door shut, leaning backwards, stretching his back out and apparently feeling every bit of his age. He leaned against the car and patted his pockets. Charlie could only imagine he was looking for cigarettes. When Lindvall didn't find what he needed, he looked back seeing everything on the rear of the counter and realized he needed to go back and get them and probably his wallet.

Charlie was feeling pretty good for all of about ten seconds until the door to the squad car looked like it had exploded open. A still somewhat wobbly Raul stumbled out standing up looking around and then waited a second sitting back down on the seat and bringing his feet up, so he had his hands in front of him in case he fell. By the time Lindvall had turned back Raul was already racing away into an alleyway. Charlie was sure that Raul was already making plans to either go after Candace, Lindvall, or if Raul found out that Charlie had lied to him he'd be going after Charlie. Charlie sent her a text but didn't know if or when she'd seen it. He'd figured she would have sent his picture by now but didn't think that was necessary since he had gotten more than a few good looks at her stalker.

Mr. Waiter would definitely be seeing a dentist though if he survived this interaction with Jim. He obviously had not forgotten about that little love tap on his still very sore and healing shoulder. As soon as the man yelled, the other two men kicked their chairs back, spinning around pulling their pistols, aiming them directly in Jim's direction. Jim in three quick succession of punches struck the guy with the handcuffs in the temple, the nose, and once again in the teeth. He looked like he was about to drop when Jim spun him around putting his would-be waiter in front, using him as a human shield.

He seriously hoped that these two pricks liked the waiter prick enough to not shoot him just to kill Jim. Unfortunately, Tim was still sitting there and waiting very impatiently to be released from his vulnerable state of captivity. Tim was saying a few prayers, seriously hoping that he was not going to be collateral damage caught in the crossfire. What he really wanted and what he got much like in life were two completely different things.

Jim ran his free hand down the man's side, happy that he was a gangster douchebag that tucked his pistol in the rear of his pants belt line. He pulled the gun without hesitation, making sure there was no safety that needed flipped or a hammer that needed pulled back. Jim fired off three shots without any hesitation or warning. Unlike them, Jim could give a fuck if these guys were alive or not after they had kidnapped the two of them.

Jim already knew damn well that he was well within his legal rights after being drugged and kidnapped to take care of the son of a bitches. He shot both men in the gut and one in the leg. Jim still thought about shooting this prick but in hindsight decided Mr. Waiter just didn't need to be awake. He took the gun, flipped it around, and smashed him over the head with the butt of the pistol. The man's knees gave out instantly and he fell down hard, smacking his head on the side of a table and when he hit the ground his still heavily bleeding mouth began to paint a silhouette around his head. The concrete floor turned a dark crimson color quickly that the man would wake up in if he was lucky enough to wake again.

The two men were writhing in pain on the ground. Jim walked over and the two of them still had their pistols clutched in their hands. But the unquestionable agonizing pain they were feeling made doing anything with them merely impossible. Jim yelled, "Toss your guns now, towards me."

The two of them hesitated, knowing that if they didn't have guns that there was no guarantee there'd be a future for them, once they did. Jim was running short on patience but knew from the weight of the gun that there were plenty of bullets left. Jim fired off two more shots, shooting each of them in the leg; for the one on the right, it was a second hole in his leg. They both screamed in agony. The two of them screamed, thinking it'd work or that by some chance he'd care, "No Inglés, No Inglés, No Inglés."

Jim smiled, thinking he should have been in foreign relations because after he'd fired off the two additional shots, each of them waved their guns and tossed them aside. Jim held up the handcuffs and pointed to the lock. One of the men fought and pulled out a set of keys. He tossed them to Jim and began screaming, "Llamar a un doctor, Llamar a un doctor, Llamar a un doctor."

Jim smiled realizing he was wasting time and knew they were asking for him to call a doctor but couldn't help himself. Jim didn't fill them at ease when he said, "Estarás bien, mi gato está aquí." Meaning you will be okay my cat is here.

The two men were sure that he'd let them die happily. Jim looked at the table seeing the men's cell phones there. He held them up before tossing them to the other side of the room. Tim screamed, "Quit fucking around. There's got to be more guys here!"

Jim grabbed the tossed pistols. He wasn't dying to see if they would go for the guns or the phones. Getting shot multiple times by two very pissed off, scary Columbian figures was not his highest priority at the moment. Jim pushed the worktable in front of the door that opened inwards, knowing nobody from the outside was going to be able to budge that damn thing.

He ran over to Tim, sorting through the keys until he found one that looked like a handcuff key and used the knife he'd procured from the guy to slice the zip ties. It wasn't as sexy as picking the locks, but it was quick, and they needed to move. Tim immediately wasted no time putting a hand out for the pistol. Jim, who not in a million years would have expected to hear this as he handed over the gun and Tim said, "I can't believe it's you that saved my life."

Jim said, "And here I was expecting a big wet one. And you

know, a little thank you, even."

Tim, lightning quick, grabbed onto both sides of Jim's face, gripping it tightly. Jim could not have been more in shock when Tim, who was the straightest guy he'd ever met leaned in and gave him a giant kiss on the lips before spinning a very shocked Irishman around, slapping him on the ass. Tim screamed, "Let's get the fuck out of here!"

Chapter 14

Charlie had not wasted any time with heading back to Fratto's house and requesting a favor. He did not think that he would get a no answer, but it was difficult to gauge sometimes if someone was going to say yes or say no. This time had been a whole heartedly yes along with the news that he had already made the call for Charlie to try to grease the wheels of local government to make sure he got his license, before he was as old as Fratto.

Fratto had asked him if he needed any assistance, and as much as Charlie thought having someone on his back might be a good idea, if it wasn't someone that he knew how to work with, he wasn't sure long term how great that would be for himself. He sped like a bat out of hell back to the boat and saw Johnney sitting in a chair staring at something off of the engine. Johnney was multi-tasking amazingly and was as busy looking as he was drinking a cold beer. Charlie said, "Johnney, I think it's time to get the boat put back together."

Johnney held up a finger apparently dead set that he needed to polish off the entire beer which he did like a champ. Johnney said, "I'll have you back up and going in three hours, lickety split."

Charlie's jaw dropped and before he could mutter the words 'three hours' Johnney broke into a smile saying, "Nah, I'm just fucking with ya. Why don't ya give me ten minutes. I'll put this shit back on. It looks like a lot, but it's just the cover and a couple of things that I don't even know what the hell they do. But the boat will be alright, it just needs a couple minutes."

"That sounds a hell of a lot better than three hours."

"Yeah, well I'll do my best. Now just remember I'm not going with. I mean, you had to have seriously pissed off some guys."

Charlie gave a thumbs up; he wasn't terribly upset that he would not be joining him. Charlie replied, "I think this one's probably better if you sit it out, Johnney. I quite frankly don't have the first clue what is going on once I get to wherever the hell I'm going. What do you mean I pissed off some guys?"

"Well, a couple guys showed up with a truck that looked like someone covered it in gasoline and lit it on fire. The thing looks like shit and is probably brand new...at least it was brand new."

Charlie tried not to cringe as the words made their way to his ear holes. He looked over his shoulder nonchalantly, noticing that the once very nice vehicle had definitely and without question taken a good amount of depreciation off pretty quickly. Charlie said, "Any chance you might be able to get this done a little quicker? Not trying to speed you up or anything but I have a feeling some shit might be hitting the fan."

"Oh, so I get the joy of putting this all back together right and then you jump on the boat, haul ass out of here and then I gotta go walk back up there. I'm assuming that truck or Escalade or whatever the fuck those things are fancy ass Cadillacs for yuppies, and I get to deliver the bad news when they ask me where you went?"

Charlie really, really didn't want to offer this but he kind of figured he didn't really have a whole lot of choice about it, morally. Charlie said, "You know Johnney, it might be smart if you come with me."

"Am I gonna die?"

"Well, I can't really say yes or no either way. But I can assure you that walking back up there without any guns could be an issue…"

Charlie had a lot on his mind and had forgotten but quickly was reminded by Johnney when he pulled the old twelve gauge out that he'd brought along with his tools. Johnney had a confident smile when he set it on the top of the deck saying, "And it's loaded with one in the chamber. I barely even got a buzz, so I could still lay it down if I needed to."

"It still might not be the worst idea if you come with me, Johnney. It is your call, man. I'd just feel horrible if anything happened to you."

Johnney was thinking that he was starting to not like this boat as much as he had when it didn't really have any stink attached that went along with it. He said, "Well, I still need a couple minutes to get this shit back on. You get your ass moving. Get everything turned on with the electric system so she's ready to roll."

Charlie nodded, putting the large duffel case over the side of the boat before climbing up on board getting ready to do exactly what he said he would. Four doors opened on the Escalade and what Charlie had originally for whatever reason assumed was an empty SUV minus the one person behind the wheel very much turned out not to be the case at all. Charlie saw the men realized that Johnney was putting the boat back together and was doing it quickly.

Charlie could understand why they were upset about the car. However, he figured they should have been all right with it getting put back together given they needed him to use a boat, unless they thought that Charlie had a helicopter stuck up his ass. His current likeability meter was leaning towards the low side. There was a pretty strong chance overall that he might have pissed them off.

Johnney said, "Can we not try to do any of them acronym things with your name today?"

Charlie had no idea what he was talking about. Charlie said, "What the hell are you talking about?"

"You know Ford…Found on roadside dead, get it? I'm just saying you probably don't want to end up that way, right?"

"No. I mean, if we can avoid it, I think that would probably be best for everyone."

"Well good, because I swear between you and your Uncle Joe I have to question your sense of wanting to live to a ripe old age. You've got a hell of a head start on your uncle to kicking the bucket early. But he also started a little later in life with his chosen final profession."

"Yeah, well I really don't know what to say to that, Johnney. I have every inclination that I would like to live for quite a while."

"All right then, that's what I like to hear. Now do I need to take care of those guys with a shotgun, or is this something you think you might be able to assist with and buy us some time?"

Charlie couldn't actually say that he was a hundred percent sure about his answer. He had only gotten a glimpse of the guys that were coming down the docks. Charlie motioned for Johnney to keep going about his business and started his walk up to the four guys that were walking straight towards him with a purpose. A pissed off purpose.

Charlie still knew he had a job that they thought he was going to do. So, he figured that was probably the only reason that he did not have a set of four guys walking towards him armed to the teeth with guns in their hands ready to kill. Charlie approached somewhat slowly. He wasn't ignorant and quite frankly knew that four on one with guns was pretty shitty but that he might just take his chances when it came to dealing with these thugs one on one.

Charlie was still anxiously waiting to hear from Cliff and did not want to miss that call. He knew that things could quite easily go to shit very quickly. So, when Charlie walked up, he had his hands out, not in a fighting manner at all but just ready, knowing his hands in his pockets weren't really good for anything but keeping them warm, and down in the Keys today that was not going to be an issue. Charlie didn't know if the first guy was the driver or not because they all looked equally perturbed by him.

Charlie tried to smile, but it didn't feel like one of those warm inviting situations. Charlie knew he didn't really have much of an option because the boat wasn't ready. The truck was on the other side of these guys, and he wasn't necessarily dying to just leave Johnney to fend for himself. So, when he got up to the men, Charlie said, "Did you guys know that you can't park here without a parking pass?"

Still no smile. Charlie was thinking these four just aren't gonna be any fun at all. But he pointed to a sign and unfortunately for the first guy for whatever reason he actually did turn around looking at a sign that did not necessarily exist. Charlie was already winding up one hell of a throw. He swung, not leaving any room or question for if he was trying to do damage except when he struck him the man's jaw barely moved an inch. Charlie whispered, "Fuck me."

The man smiled, wiggling his tongue, spitting out a tooth and reached to grip onto Charlie. Charlie was trying to think on his feet about how to keep the four of these guys not circled around him so they could quite literally kick the shit out of him which didn't sound like the best idea. He also thought there was no quick way back out of the water once you entered it. The man said, "Why don't you come with us so we can have a talk."

Charlie shook his head no, making the man realize that this

little shit wasn't going to be grabbed and he wasn't going to come peacefully. Charlie rolled his neck trying to get ready for the inevitable and when the man swung this time with a pretty impressive amount of force that was when Charlie ducked again but with the exception this time he bobbed and weaved down coming up hard with an uppercut and his uppercut simply landed directly in the family jewels.

He was pretty sure the two of them were not going to be having cervezas and laughing about this later. The man's eyes crossed, and his knees began to quiver as a lone drip of drool came out. When the guy closest began to reach over to help him, that was when Charlie took him by the suit coat. He threw the swollen ball guy off the dock and into the water. The man dipped below the waterline. Charlie would have been perfectly content if the guy just drowned. But so long as he was out of his hair for a minute, Charlie could live with that. The last thing he wanted to have happen was to take another horrible beating.

The helper guy looked up with surprise, apparently he hadn't expected Charlie to toss who he could only assume was his boss into the water. The three of them had to question if he'd gotten hit hard enough to just not come back up. Charlie quite frankly didn't give a shit. He figured if this was how they were going to try and treat him four on one that there really wasn't much of a limit when it came to what he would do back to them.

Charlie wasn't going to waste even a second. The helper guy didn't predict what was coming, and he also didn't see one quick jab flying straight to his jugular, smashing his windpipe, and he instantly began to wheeze sounding like a smoker with asthma. Charlie held the guy up in front of him trying to use him as a makeshift shield until the two men that were with him, who he could only assume apparently weren't the biggest fans of him, took the guy by his suit coat and threw him into the water and out of the way. The throat punch guy tried to keep his balance, but once they threw him he went straight into the water falling on swollen balls guy as well. Both of them went under the water.

Charlie was thinking maybe the back two guys were the muscles. One guy was a boss, or a driver, and he thought maybe this guy was just someone's nephew. The two came after Charlie at once, both reaching for him, and he knew this was probably bad. Charlie felt around in his pockets, not really wanting to bring out a knife and kill these guys. He couldn't actually think of a very good reason why he shouldn't just kill them and be done, but alas that was what he thought, and that was what he was going to do. Charlie caught the glistening of his belt coming off his buckle. Charlie thought that it was a nice, still painful but not deadly, alternative to murdering them. Charlie pulled off his belt as quick as he could, backing up, still trying to keep away from the giant claws of death that were reaching for him. He waited until they reached at the right time before looping his belt around their wrists, making it tight and creating a gangster leash.

Charlie pulled back as hard as he could, but the two men had a suspicion that Charlie was going to try and pull. Charlie was no match for the two of them…or even one of them pulling back. Charlie had expected their reaction and quite frankly couldn't have been happier. He wanted to get the hell out of there and this was going to be that perfect reason why he could. Charlie was just a little bit smarter than these guys and the moment that they started using their force to pull backwards was the moment that Charlie simply let go, actually surprising them by running up, jumping midair and putting both feet up. He used their momentum to connect with their sternums and sent them back stumbling into the water.

The look of surprise on the two men was priceless, and Charlie couldn't say he was overly upset about how that worked out. He thought, compared to Bruno and Lou and the gang, that that was definitely a much better turn of events than their first meeting in the boat. Although he still held true today that if he had his chance and had known they were coming and not just broken in, that he might have been able to put up a pretty decent fight. Charlie turned around; he didn't need to stand and gloat. It was time to get the fuck out of there and to do it quickly. He raced back to the boat.

Johnney was just putting the finishing touches on the boat. He yelled to Charlie, "I thought we wanted to get the hell out of here?"

"I do, but there's not a lot of getting to be done when we have those four guys that could have ran and jumped onto the boat. I still don't know what the hell they want, and quite frankly, at this point, I'm not interested in finding out."

Johnney shrugged, throwing his tools up onto the deck. Charlie winced a little bit when he saw some fresh scratches on it, but he knew at the same time today would not have been an ideal day to try and get a boat mechanic to come out and sit and do nothing. Although he did think hey that would have been a pretty damn easy paycheck for somebody, especially if they were thirsty.

Charlie raced down, flipping the switches, giving them a minute, and powering the boat up. Johnney was getting the boat unhooked from its lines and realized he was too old for this shit and that the kid should be the one here doing it. That, of course, was not actually an option right now so that is not how things went down. Charlie watched, waiting for him to get his feet up just enough that he was on board and able for him to punch the gas. The men were finally getting out of the water; only the smaller throat punch guy had been able to get out first by pulling himself up. Charlie figured that the rest of them probably had to swim down to where there was a ladder which he knew wasn't close.

As soon as the men had gotten out of the water they began racing towards Charlie's boat. The smaller man that had taken the strike to the throat earlier had been the fastest and more than likely lightest out of all of them. He made it to the boat just in time to leap from the edge of the dock and from there was barely able to catch the edge of the railing. He looked down at the water seeing the giant engines that were making instant waves immediately and held on as tight as he could, turning his fingers and knuckles white, not daring to let go and knowing he was going down if he did in the water for a second time.

Johnney noticed him running towards the dock and leaping. Johnney rolled over, pushing himself up all at once, or at least tried to do it all at once. The twenty-year-old Johnney showed up every once in a while, except his knees which had drastically different opinions. He had to catch his own balance, holding onto the railing as one knee and then the other gave out under him. It didn't help that the boat was going up and down. Johnney saw Charlie trying to say something but couldn't hear him over the engines and the man screaming. Johnney shrugged looking through the window to Charlie who screamed 'Get him the fuck off!'

Johnney gave a thumbs up trying to keep his balance and put up his foot kicking the man in one hand, and when he tried to lift his foot a second time, the man disappeared into the water below. Charlie would have felt bad if he hadn't thought these guys were with the Colombian mob that was trying to really fuck up his day. He'd had pretty high expectations of this day

not being nearly as shitty as this, especially after getting to

meet Candace and getting a good look at her. He could see

potential for why anyone would think that she was something

special. Of course, he wouldn't be all stalkery about it. He

figured if he did try to pursue that further, one issue would be

her trusting men again. He truly hoped that Raul hadn't

ruined something so wonderful with his actions.

Charlie looked in the water, seeing the man was okay and

looked like he was doing a pretty shitty back float and trying

to get himself moving back towards the shore. He could only

imagine the waves this boat made and having to try and fight

his way through the massive waves that it was creating.

Johnney came in, plopping down on the seat behind the wheel

next to Charlie. Johnney cracked a beer rubbing his knees

before he cracked it. "Well, surprisingly this isn't all that much

different than the last time. It's nice to know that anytime you

guys need to do something you need to do it at full fucking

throttle. It's a character statement really, glad that you guys

have kept me alive so far. I won't lie. It's probably pretty good

that that guy fell off because I don't know if my leg was gonna

go up that high a second time. I was pretty damn sure I would

fall off the boat if I had to try and keep that balance for any amount of time."

Charlie slowed the boat down. They were a safe distance from his dock and Charlie saw that Cliff was trying to call. Charlie motioned for Johnney to take the wheel and hit answer on the phone. He said, "Cliff, is that you?"

"Yeah it's me. You really pissed off whoever that guy was outside. He looked like a fucking psychopath."

"No, he doesn't look like one."

"I think he does."

"I just meant he doesn't look like one. He is one. He is batshit crazy, and he's actually going to be my first paid case."

"Wasn't that Lindvall guy giving you shit about not working until you got yourself a license?"

"Well, if you had seen the girl that hired me, you probably wouldn't have said no either. I guess I'm just a sucker for a pretty face."

Cliff couldn't say anything to retort. He was absolutely in no way better when it came to himself and how hard he had fallen for his girlfriend Chandra. He replied, "I get it, stuff wiggles between my legs too."

"Thanks for that lovely thought, Cliff. I was really hoping one day I would have the opportunity to picture you naked, and well, now I've had it."

"You're welcome. My girlfriend thinks I have got the prettiest black ass in the world, just in case you were curious."

"Yeah I wasn't, thanks though. Now I've got a whole third thing going in my head. As much as I am enjoying this conversation I would like to know…did you find them?"

"Yeah, that's why I called."

"All right, where are they?"

The last visual that I had of them was when a boat docked about 20 miles east of where you dock. I won't bore you with details you won't understand but I hacked into a security company and now I've got video of a bunch of guys making a shaky trip trying to get Jim and Tim back to the building. I'm pretty sure they are still there."

"So, they're in a building and they're not in a boat? But they are still kidnapped?"

"Yeah you got it, boss. Is there anything else that you need me to do?"

Charlie was shaking his head no. He really couldn't think of anything else that Cliff could do that wouldn't put his life in danger. He was trying his damndest to not make too long of a list of people that might die because they were associated with him. Charlie said, "If you can just send me where they're at I'll cut you loose."

"Are you sure you don't want a computer guy available?"

"What exactly would a computer guy do, Cliff?"

"Well maybe you want to know before you go around a corner if there's a camera there and if someone is ready to shoot you in the side of the head or has a baseball bat or pliers or…"

"Yeah I get it. Lots of pain, lots of pain that could be inflicted on myself. Well, let's hope that it doesn't come down to that. But if you don't mind hanging out at Starbucks for just a little bit longer then I will happily keep you working until I get my buddies back."

"All you have to do is ask. I'm not gonna lie. I feel a little guilty taking three hundred bucks from ya. I mean, this job wasn't really all that hard in the first place. So, you know, I don't want you to feel like I ripped you off."

"Well, sometimes when someone thinks something is easy, it could not possibly be a shittier job for another person. So, hey, don't even worry about it. It is no big deal. You keep your phone handy though, I may or may not need some help. In the meantime, why don't you see if there's any cameras on the inside of that building if that's something you can do? If not, it's all good. Just kind of figure it out as I go."

"Try not to get yourself killed, Charlie."

"Yeah, that's kind of the plan at hand."

"Sounds like a pretty good plan to have."

Charlie definitely didn't have any intentions of today being his last on Earth. He knew when people were under stress that they could make mistakes and he knew that mistakes could kill you. However, Charlie still wasn't worried. He just figured that everything somehow would work out in the end. He didn't know why he thought that because he was going in blind, but he could try a million things to see if they work. It wouldn't hurt a bit.

Chapter 15

The Jim and Tim duo had not wasted any amount of time when it came to deciding if they should barricade themselves inside before they would have to worry about whoever was on the other side of that door trying to make his or her way in. The two knew that unless someone was deaf or stupid that it wouldn't take a genius to figure out those were gunshots being fired off. Additionally, since neither of them spoke Spanish for shit, they couldn't really say anything back when the radio chatter basically had begun immediately. That chatter that neither could understand had only ramped up and from their tone sounded angrier the second they tried opening the door and couldn't budge it open.

Jim asked, "Do you have any ideas at all? I mean I always have to come up with all the good ideas. So, what do you got? Do we just open up the door and start firing off like crazy bastards?"

"No, I can't say if that seems like we're gonna live if we do that, Jim. Besides, you're kind of a shitty shot."

"That hurts, Tim. It really hurts."

"You shot both those guys in the gut."

"Well, that's a good thing."

"Why would that be a good thing?"

"Because that's where I was aiming. I wasn't necessarily trying to go out of my way to kill them, but I did want to make sure they weren't a threat any longer."

Tim looked at the two men. One of them was definitely moving a lot slower than the other. But, they were headed to try and retrieve the phones Jim had tossed. Tim asked, "What exactly are you expecting to have happened? If they actually call 911 and not just a gigantic Colombian hit squad to come here? You realize now you're going to get perfectly innocent EMTs that are just out trying to help good people get shot because of it."

Jim did not like admitting when he had possibly not fully thought out a seemingly full-fledged plan. He said, "Should we take them with us, and we can leave them out front? Maybe we could put a sticky note on their foreheads saying abdomen gunshot?"

"You do know you're an idiot, right?"

"You know what my mom says?"

"Yeah, that she always wants seconds…"

"Goddamnit that that was a good one. Damn it, I hate walking into those. She does think I'm smart though. It does annoy me that she finds you handsome. Oh, and I will kill you if you touch my mom."

Tim said, "Did you happen to see our stuff anywhere?"

Jim was shaking his head no. Tim said, "Well then maybe you should go get one of those phones and call Charlie. Or you could call the cops. I'm sure they'll arrest us for shooting two men that kidnapped us and drugged us and then tied us to chairs but at least we will be out of here."

"Yeah I think if that Lindvall guy comes he's not going to be super happy to see us. I'd actually be surprised if he came once someone told him who it was. Are they allowed to do that? Like not to come and not help us?"

"If anyone's going to come up with an excuse, Jim, it's going to be Lindvall."

Jim said, "How about we just get out of here? Call Charlie, call the cops, call medical services and let them know what's going on and that we think a police presence needs to be here when they show up."

Tim actually liked the idea, not that he was going to tell Jim that. He and the three of them basically went out of their way to make sure they didn't pay too many compliments to one another. Nobody wanted to get big heads and it was just one of those guy code things that they all took pretty damn seriously.

The door continued pounding and at some point that table which Jim had pushed in front of it apparently had had enough weight put on it that it was starting to budge. Tim ran around the room. He knew there had to be something they could do to either keep that door shut or make it so that nobody wanted to enter this place. With as much force as was getting pushed on the door there was nothing to keep it from coming open. When Tim kicked up some sawdust he realized this could have been a carpenter shop or maybe the sawdust was just to soak up the blood of all the people they brought here and killed. He was hoping that the latter was not the case. He found a screwdriver and pried off a padlock from one of the double cabinets that was quite wide.

There was an air compressor hose and all kinds of different power drills in there. Tim saw a torch as well but did not feel confident enough in his knowledge of how one works to not get himself killed. Jim looked over to see what he was doing, and he who had been in the mechanic pool in the Navy was more than excited to see that torch. He said, "Can you buy me some time while I get that torch set up?"

Jim had absolutely no idea if Tim could buy him any time. If he could, Jim wondered how much time, or what the hell he was going to do if he did get that time. Tim said, "What do you want me to do? Start shooting through the door hole?"

Jim shrugged, "I've heard worse ideas today. What else is in there?"

Tim gave a look saying, "Drills, staplers, nail guns…"

Jim's eyes lit up when he said nail gun. He smiled with nothing which would be good intentions for anyone besides them. Jim said, "Winner winner chicken dinner. That's the one we want. Get the compressor plugged in and flip that bitch. That thing is heavy duty, it won't take any time to fill that tank."

"Do you really think a nail gun is gonna kill someone?"

Jim said, "You seem hung up on killing everyone. I'm fine not killing them. All you need to do is just put a fresh strip of nails in that thing and run it up and down until whoever is trying to get in decides to stop and that it hurts more than is worth the effort."

Tim was okay with this idea and hauled the 300-gallon air compressor over to the wall plugging it in to get it filling up and ran back to get his new weapon. Tim waited and patiently got everything connected watching Jim in the corner throwing on what looked like a hockey mask and somewhat looked a little bit too frightfully like Jason. Jim yelled, "Just give me a couple minutes. I think that we will be okay."

"Yeah , trapped on the inside of a room with no windows and people trying to kill us. What could possibly go wrong with one of your plans?"

Jim said, "Just shut up. I'll make it so that door won't open for anything short of a damn battering ram."

"So, how do we get out? I mean once you get us trapped in the windowless room."

Tim could tell instantly that aspect hadn't crossed Jim's whatever size mind. Jim's shoulders sunk a little bit but when he looked at the box of nails next to him, Tim saw that each strip of nails held three hundred and he thought that hey I've got a hell of a lot of ammo before I need to refill. The tank turned off after it had filled, and an evil smile appeared on Tim's face.

He checked the thing over, placing the gun on auto and when the door opened just enough for a hand to go through, Tim realized this poor bastard was going to get it worse than anyone. He jammed the guy's hand up next to the wall and let out three nails on three different parts of his palm. A scream and a language he didn't understand but he was pretty sure it was the Spanish word for shit and fuck me echoed through the door.

The man was trying while never stopping screaming to get his palm free. Tim put the nail gun up where the man's head would be and ran a string of shots directly down the entire width of the doorframe top to bottom. Hole in the hand guy was not alone and his screams echoed even over the sound of the air compressor kicking back on as it sucked in fresh air for Tim's seemingly never-ending machine-gun nailer.

Tim looked at how long the connection hose from the tank to the gun was and knew he could probably go twenty or thirty feet before he needed to be worried about running out of hose. He figured at that point It would be an excellent time to just switch over to the gun. Jim had already come back asking, "So what are we going to do?"

Tim said, "I'm going to put a fresh strip of nails in this bitch and then you're going to slide the table back so we can open the door. I'm going to unleash a whole 'nother string of nails. I'm going to refill the damn thing and then I'm going to rinse and repeat, how's that fucking sound?"

"It sounds like our chances of dying have decreased, probably like five percent," Jim said.

"Better down than up," Tim said as he did exactly as he said he would. By the time he was done, only the man whose hand was nailed to the wall was left. The guy was screaming in agony but at least he was outside the door. Tim was pretty confident that whoever found the first pair of needle nose pliers was going to be the most favorite person in the whole wide world.

After Tim loaded a fresh round of 300 nails in the gun, he gathered all of the hose and waited until Jim slid the table enough so the two could get out. As soon as they did, the man who had more nails than anyone would want to count or in his case probably be needing to have pulled out was barely conscious. Jim was holding his pistol by the barrel ready to hit him over the head, but Tim shook his head no. The man thought about the pistol in his hand for a second. He realized the end game for him wasn't going to be killing these guys. He dropped the pistol on the ground. He was done fighting for today. The hand nail guy who may or may not have known much English sure as shit knew what a universal head shake meant, and he simply said, "Gracias."

They made it all of about a foot into the hallway before a horde of fresh men came out from around the corner. Their intentions were clear with their guns up. Before they had all gotten in place so they wouldn't shoot each other in the head, Tim had already been more than ready. He held down with the rapid release trigger that he couldn't think of a single reason who the hell would need to nail this many times, but by God, he loved whoever that inventor was. Tim dropped down, not necessarily wanting to get shot in the head if they did finally shoot. By the time they did get their guns up and ready. Jim said, "What the fuck are you doing?"

Tim had already fired off 50 of his nails by that time and the men's jeans and slacks had begun to turn a crimson color in the shins and thighs. Furthermore, it helped to figure out where he hit them because all of the men seemed to almost miraculously and immediately lose their sense of balance. Jim figured there was probably a pretty good chance that someone with a nail through their bone would probably have those kinds of reactions happen to them.

Tim checked over his shoulder. Jim already had his hands up looking apologetically. Tim looked back around and anyone that had not already thrown their gun had his nail gun pointed directly at them. Tim could only and would only be so kind before he decided that he wasn't going to be Mr. Nice Guy. They walked up, realizing he could only carry so many guns. Tim yelled, "How many of you are there?"

When no one answered he got about a foot away from a man yelling, "How many are there, I said, God dammit?"

The man simply replied, "No Inglés, no inglés!"

Tim placed the barrel of the gun up next to the man's bicep and looked at the guy next to him firing three nails in three different spots on his arm. The bicep nail catcher man began crying and screaming, yelling for him to stop in Spanish.

Tim looked at and had never taken his eye off of nail catcher number two. He slowly began moving the barrel of the nail gun over and placing it square on his chest. Tim was ready to say how many when the man blurted it out, "Ten, there's ten, ten!"

Tim pushed the gun into his chest a little harder, tilting his head left and right as if he wasn't quite sure that he believed him. The man wasn't going to take any chances he screamed, "Okay, okay, fuck, thirteen, there's thirteen, don't shoot me again."

While Tim had been busy making sure they got what they needed, Jim had disassembled and removed magazines and put the slide of the guns in his cargo shorts, thinking it would be damn difficult for them to shoot them in the back with guns that didn't have the slide.

Jim said, "So, let's take care of the baker's dozen and get the fuck out of here."

"You've never had such a good idea."

"Well, I think getting out of the cuffs and freeing us was a pretty good idea. But don't you think I need a big smooch every time my genius shines through? I don't usually kiss on the first date."

"That was a one-time thing, and I've seen you kiss before you knew their name. Let's find anyone who still wants to keep us here and get them out of the way."

Chapter 16

Charlie did a drive by the place that Cliff had sent him. He saw the boats out front definitely didn't belong there. They were probably as expensive as the boat Charlie was cruising along in, but these ones were more than likely only for doing bad things. Cliff answered and he said, "Do you need anything else? What is up, I got your eyes and stuff."

"Do you know how to block a cell phone?"

"Why?"

"Because I am going to get my friends out of there. If I know them, they are going to cause as much hell as possible for whoever the poor bastards dealing with them are. I am sure that they will give them back…or kill them, hard to say."

"So, I do know how, but the problem is I don't own a jammer."

"How much would it cost for you to own one?"

"Well, I don't want to own…"

"Okay, remember the life and death thing I was talking about. That's still on the table. I don't want to do anything that will put their lives in danger. What I plan on doing isn't quite on the table for what I was asked to do. But I don't take orders from pieces of shits and that's not going to change today. How quickly could you get one and be at that location?"

"I thought the idea was not to put me in any danger at all. Like to keep me out of harm's way this time."

"Look, you drop that thing off and drive away, how does that sound? I will happily reimburse you for the scrambler thing. Just get a receipt or something to be honest just tell me what it costs. I don't think you'd screw me over."

"If you die?"

Charlie was starting to feel more than a bit annoyed. He couldn't necessarily blame the guy for not wanting to get shot at…again. But he needed help. Charlie said, "Tell ya what, write this card number down. You can order it online and pick it up at the curb. You'll be Mr. Charlie Ford for a few minutes and luckily for you if I die then you get a free jammer and you don't have to worry about being reimbursed. How soon can you get to that spot?"

"How soon do you need..."

"As soon as fucking possible, please. You could say that time is definitely of the essence here."

"I don't know, maybe twenty minutes. How does that sound?"

"Like I need to reimburse you for a speeding ticket as well. I'll see you in twenty or less…preferably less. Just call me when you get there."

Cliff hit end on his phone; he had already tossed the item in his cart and was paying with his new persona of Mr. Charlie Ford. He didn't waste any time and figured that he'd feel bad getting paid if it just ended up with him getting murdered alongside his buddies. This wasn't something that he thought he would be okay with.

Johnney said, "So, how did that one go? It sounds like you had to pay for your stuff with a credit card. Does that mean that you bought some more help for this?"

"It means that their help won't know what is going on. All we need to do is go around the shore a few times. I need to make sure that their help that isn't here doesn't know what is going on. Can you drive the boat, drop me off and then we'll call you as soon as I get them out."

"You got an extra phone?"

"I'll call you. What is your number?"

"To the office?"

"To your cell."

"What cell?"

"You don't have a phone."

"Yeah, I use the one at the office."

"Why don't you have a cell?"

"Well, why the fuck would I need one? I got an office phone. I don't order out and I ain't got no or want no girlfriend. Not much reason to have one unless I want to be like all of them kids out there who just stare at those things until the end of fucking time like some moron."

Charlie couldn't necessarily disagree with the fact that he who was still pushing to get to thirty couldn't stand the majority of teens and early twenty somethings walking around. Jesus could be walking down the street turning overpriced coffees into wine with a wave of his hand and no one would be the wiser. Charlie sighed because he really wanted to make as quick of a getaway as possible. Charlie wasn't really sure what the answer was, but common sense kicked in and he said, "How's this for a crazy idea, how about you wait until you see me, a giant black guy, and a giant red headed Irishman and then you come down and pick us up just about as god damn quickly as you possibly can? How does that sound to you?"

"Well now, it sounds like my chances of getting shot at are going up pretty quickly."

Charlie reached under the seat showing him a pair of binoculars saying, "Look, you drop me off a half mile down. I'll make my way up and once we get out of there if the heat's on us you'll see us running down the dock like a bat out of hell. We're all pretty good swimmers you know, so long as we don't have cement shoes. Once we do that then you come pick us up."

"You realize the scenario where you guys are running like a bat out of hell down the docks is the one which I am least excited about right?"

"Well Johnney, I would have to say that that makes two of us, compadre."

Johnney said, "You know what little relationship I had with your uncle seems like it had been far less dangerous than this one. Oh, and that isn't a compliment."

"Well, that would have been a weird compliment if it was, Johnney. So, how about you get me over to the next set of docks down from this one and I'll take myself a little jog."

"Aren't you gonna wait for Cliff to do his thing?"

Charlie held up the phone saying, "Well this useless thing here is also good for sending messages and getting information. Cliff already said that he dropped off the scrambler with fresh batteries in it and that I should be in the clear to at least not have to worry about them trying to call out for help."

"Hey buttercup, you realize that goes both ways, right? Shit hits the fan on the inside of that place and you get stuck in there. There ain't no calling the cops. You're just gonna be screwed."

"Well hopefully, if things go bad then I can just take one to the back of the head. I prefer to not have to worry about being chopped up with chainsaws. It would make such a mess."

"You're a little morbid aren't ya?"

"No more than anyone else is."

"Not sure about that, best get your ass out there though."

Charlie was timing when the boat was going to be close enough for him to do a running jump so Johnney could just turn the boat around and head back out of sight. Charlie took a few steps back from the edge of the deck. When it was close enough, he took off in a dead sprint. He didn't waste any time when the boat was close enough. Johnney was already turning the wheel and heading back out before Charlie's feet touched the ground. He took off running, not wasting the time he didn't have. He wasn't very close before his leg began to vibrate. Charlie had originally thought it would've taken Cliff longer but true to his word he truly had driven like a bat out of hell. Charlie was kind of proud of him. Charlie sent a simple message back saying "Thanks, now get out of this shit zone now."

A reply came almost immediately saying, "No worries, I'm miles away."

Charlie was going to respond with something along the lines of being a smartass because that's how he rolled. However, he looked down and to his satisfaction his screen started looking like a TV from the 80s when the cable went out. Nothing but a white and black fuzz started to appear on his screen. Charlie smiled feeling the adrenaline pumping him up but at the exact same time couldn't stop thinking about the words from Johnney reminding him that the shit hitting the fan went both ways and both ways was not good if he got in a bad situation.

Charlie tucked the now useless phone away. There wasn't a helluva lot it was going to do at the moment, so he decided to replace that with a pistol. Charlie looked around the area, thinking about where he'd look around the area from if it was him. He kept out of view, seeing the top of the building had a guy with a machine gun sitting up top. Like anyone who'd been at a job for a while and for hours the excitement of it sure seemed to wear off.

Charlie made his way over to the main building. He looked around, finding somewhere to be able to climb up. He waited for the man to turn around and raced up behind him saying, "Nothing personal, here."

The guy turned around with the gun up. Charlie was already swinging his fist. It connected directly with his throat, and he immediately began fighting for air. Charlie caught the machine gun, pulling it away from him as he fell to the ground. Charlie said, "It will go away; just give it time. You'll have plenty of it available because I'm gonna leave you up here."

The man was wheezing for breath. He still tried putting up a fight. Charlie whispered, "It didn't have to hurt, but that's up to you."

Charlie punched him in the face twice, making him question if he should hold his bleeding nose or his throat, which he could do absolutely nothing about. Charlie, being the friendly guy that he was, flipped him over checking his pockets, and seeing his phone had the same issue that his own did. This didn't break Charlie's heart. He was trying to think of his next move, but when he heard gunshots coming from below him, Charlie got a zip tie cuff that he already had made up. He pulled at them until he could see that a certain amount of circulation was being cut off from his arms to his hands. Charlie raced back to where he had climbed up.

By the time he had gotten down there and found a main door, he could hear men screaming at the tops of their lungs. Charlie didn't have a clue what in the hell was going on. The great escape that he'd conjured seemed like it was not going as planned…not whatsoever. The door slammed open, and two guys were making their way out, each of them with nails embedded in their sides and heads. Charlie almost smiled when he heard Jim yelling like a maniac as loud as he could.

Charlie raced forward, not using the gun as he dove towards both of them. The heavy metal door was not kind to them, and they felt every inch of their bodies that slammed into it. They dropped their pistols, more concerned about getting out of there than retaliation. When they tried to get up, Jim and Tim came around the corner. Jim had a gun in each of his hands and Tim looked like he was carrying a nail gun. When they saw Charlie, the two of them couldn't have had bigger shit eating grins.

Tim dropped the nail gun saying, "Who do you got with you?"

"It is just me."

Tim pinched at the bridge of his nose saying, "What in the hell does that mean it is just you? What were you going to do against that many guys? What are you, stupid?"

"Yeah, really stupid, because I figured you two might need saving. How did you get out?"

"It isn't relevant until we get out of here. How'd you get here anyway? Is the truck parked close by?"

"I brought the boat. Johnney has it right now. When we get to the docks, he's going to circle in and pick us up."

"But we gotta get those guys taken care of."

Tim said, "Most of them can't move. They've been shot many, many times with my trusty new best friend, the nail gun."

"It definitely looks like you made an impact; excuse the pun."

Jim, who was more than happy to leave, asked, "So, why was it that we needed to do this?"

"Because we still have to deal with the fact that these guys think that I'm doing something that they asked me to do."

Jim jokingly said, "So, you're saying we couldn't just take the boat and, oh yeah, all our shits already on it, and just leave? I mean, we figured out the truth with your Uncle Joe. What else do we have to stay here for?"

"I actually don't think that sounds like the worst plan, Jim. But they know who we are, and obviously they are pretty capable of being really fucking quiet, and that just kind of seems like a dangerous concoction. We don't have to stay here, but we sure as shit aren't going to leave because we are running scared. I'd rather die than sleep with one eye open."

"So, your idea is to not do what they want. Except we are going to go to where they want us to do some job?"

"The two of you aren't going anywhere. I just want to make sure that there's no loose ends here. So, that way when I go there, they don't just shoot me in the head."

Tim asked, "And there's like no way that we could possibly just see if Mr. Fratto could…you know, send his mobster army out there to meet them and kill them?"

Charlie had made quick work putting the zip ties on the bleeding men as he had found them. Charlie replied, "Fratto still seems like he's stuck in bed, but I did stop a second time today and picked up the biggest goddamn rifle I've ever seen in my life from his man in charge. So, if one of you, no offense Jim…cough cough, Tim is interested in being in a smaller boat while I head out to this location then maybe, you know, you could, I don't know, shoot a hole through their boat or body whichever one lets you sleep at night?"

Tim laughed saying, "Believe it or not, after waking up drugged and tied to a chair without a beautiful woman to surprise me, I am pretty open minded about what I would be willing to do."

Charlie said, "We can head back to the docks. How does that sound?"

"It sounds like a really good idea. It's been kind of a long day, and well, I felt like a cat at some point crapped in my mouth. I'd love a drink of water and maybe a toothbrush."

"Well, that's lovely. It sounds like a good idea."

Chapter 17

The three of them raced down to the docks. If there weren't any people following them, they didn't want to wait until one of the men got out. They were locked down pretty tight, and they couldn't see anyone coming to help them. At least that's what they were hoping for. Johnney was coming in like a bat out of hell. He slowed down, letting the men jump on deck. They barely had a second before Johnney, who looked seemingly and deservingly nervous, gunned the engine. The horsepower of the boat put them on their asses.

Johnney waited until he had that boat a good mile off the coast. The boat had been tossing the men around like ice cubes in an empty cup. They didn't get sick when it came to boats but even this was not necessarily easy on anyone. Johnney yelled from behind the wheel, "Why the hell are you all cuddling on the ground together? I thought that you boys were Navy men. Did you already lose your damn sea legs?"

Jim said, "Yeah, funny how a boat going sixty miles per hour or more, ramping off of waves, makes it difficult to, you know…get up off my ass."

"Well don't you worry, Uncle Johnney will take care of you,

now."

Jim whispered, "I don't think I want to call him Uncle Johnney."

Tim patted him on his shoulder saying, "Don't worry, just so long as you call me daddy."

Jim couldn't give him a straight look. It would seem that Tim was on his A game today. He was quite happy about the idea of the hell he was going to give Tim the next few days. They went straight back to their dock after taking a spin around looking for those men that Charlie had helped enjoy the warm waters of the Florida Keys. Charlie had brought them up to speed on the additional issues with Raul and Lindvall, being his normal dickish self which wasn't going to help anything else.

Charlie thought the boat he was in was in better fighting shape right now then the two of them. Although he could only laugh at the fact that he'd gone through all that shit just to end up mostly needing to give them a ride. But there's a reason that he had originally called them down to help him with Fratto junior's crew, aka Nydegger's crew. They had figured out that a simple boat rental for Jim and Tim to take the sniper rifle out on would be the easiest. Those plans changed instantly as he looked up at his three men's faces. There wasn't a look on anyone's face that was pleasant or like things were going well. Jim, who almost never looked nervous, was filling him with no confidence.

A hammer on a pistol cocked behind his head. Charlie had both hands on the rope and knew by the time he let go of it and turned around that more than likely he'd already have a minimum of two bullets in his head or chest. Charlie said, "What the hell do you want? Where were you?"

"How do you know I don't want to shoot you in the back of the head?"

"Because most people interested in doing that just pull the trigger. So, it seems you would want something. Are you one of the four bears that I tossed into the water earlier?"

The hammer came back down but the barrel pressed into the lower part of his skull. He said, "Yeah, and I can't say that it was overly enjoyable. If you would have just let us talk and not started fighting, we could have had a much different interaction. You could have probably saved yourself and the old man a lot of worry."

"Can I turn around if I promise not to throw you in the water...again?"

"Tell your friends that I'm not going to hurt them or you…for now. I see the old timer with his shotgun; he can just leave that where it is."

Charlie's shoulders slumped but he didn't know what else he could do. He yelled, "Hey, do you think that you guys could do me a solid and not shoot him please? Johnney, I'm mostly talking to you. I don't think that if you continue pulling that twelve-gauge things are going to go well…for me, at least. I'm sure you could smoke this guy right after, but I'd prefer it not be after I die."

Johnney seemed like he was debating this request a little bit which Charlie wouldn't lie, it hurt his feelings just a little. Johnney put up his hands as did Jim and Tim and the three came out of the cabin.

Charlie turned around slowly, not wanting to make the stranger with a gun to the back of his head nervous. Rarely did things ever go well when people were worried and pointing a gun at someone. The man was holding up his ID as were the three men from earlier who had also taken a dive. He said, "See this badge?"

Charlie read the name on it saying, "It would be difficult to miss with it being two inches away from my face, Agent Hawk. Could you kindly back it the fuck up so I can actually look at it please?"

"Jesus Christ, they really broke the mold with you didn't they? Do you not get nervous about anything?"

"Oh, don't worry, you know I'm absolutely terrified on the inside. I'll probably need to go to my safe place later, until I feel better about who I am as a person."

"Do you have friends?"

"Yeah, these guys, and I'm not looking for new ones, sorry. Look, Agent Hawk, why don't you get to it. I'm not necessarily up to date on all of the civilian laws, but I am pretty sure that throwing someone in water is not illegal."

"Okay, do you think torching a government vehicle with gasoline would be frowned upon? How about striking a federal agent, what'd that happen to run you for time in jail?"

"I just did that to a vehicle. It just happened to turn out to be a government vehicle. I mean you gotta give me a little credit, right? I mean, I'm not a complete idiot."

"That's yet to be seen. I can't say that I'm feeling real confident in your intelligence factor at the moment."

"Okay, so potentially I'm a dumb fuck. But what do you want?"

"You know, if you hadn't done that earlier we were already set to swoop in, pick up your friends and then put you guys in protective custody until this job was done."

Charlie could admit when he was wrong, not to this guy but typically in general. He couldn't say that he loved hearing the news after the fact because without the flux capacitor it didn't really do a hell of a lot of good with being able to change time. Agent Hawk continued saying, "Can you tell me anything about the Fratto family?"

"I can tell you nothing about the Fratto family."

"Because you're working for them?"

"No, because I'm not a fucking idiot. Fratto didn't have anything to do with those guys that took my friends."

"How sure are you about that?"

Charlie thought about the sniper rifle that he had gotten from Fratto. If he wanted his men dead, then giving Charlie something large enough that all he needed to do was get close with his shot to kill them probably wouldn't be a great idea.

"A hundred percent, how's that for being definitive about something?"

Agent Hawk didn't really look real upset either way. But at the same time, it was hard to tell as Charlie knew the guy was probably sick as hell of him, "What did those men that took your friends want?"

"I can only actually give you part of that answer. I still have to do the entire job. But I'd be happy to give you the location that we are going to."

"You're not going anywhere. That's where we're going to go and where your involvement in this ends. You got your friends back. We are going to overlook what happened to the guys at the shop. Whoever was going apeshit with that nail gun is a sadistic bastard."

Jim said, "Actually, I told my friend, who's not here of course, that maybe they should not have gone full auto on the gun. The nail gun that is."

"What do you mean your friend who's not here? No one else came out of there."

"Well, I guess that's the benefit of being a magician, isn't it?"

"Did he eat a lot of paint chips as a kid?" Hawk asked.

Johnney who had been pretty quiet said, "What do you mean as a kid? He puts milk on them in the morning."

Agent Hawk looked at the three men behind him, half ready to just tell them to go about their business and let these guys loose. If he didn't have a soul and ethics, he figured if they died, well the world would be a quieter place for it. But he didn't think that they probably completely deserved the repercussions of a gang war when for what they had found out none of them had ever been in a gang. They had all been discharged with honor, and quite frankly, there really wasn't a whole lot to give them a hard time about. Hawk said, "Look, you guys come with us. We're going to brief you. We have a few questions, and you're more than free to sign something saying that anything you say cannot be used against you in a court of law. So, I mean it's basically that easy."

Everyone totally did not hate the idea that they would get a paper stating that they would not have to worry about criminal repercussions. Charlie looked at the guys who all shrugged. Johnney said, "I drove a fucking boat and used binoculars. I'm allowed to have that shotgun, so do I need to go with you agent fellas?"

Hawk said, "Well, if there's any strays left behind then it might be something to consider worrying about."

Johnney hated going anywhere that he wasn't one hundred percent in complete control of. Of course, sometimes it all came down to a simple fact which was if he didn't go with someone he was going to die. That seemed like a reoccurring thing going on quite regularly with Charlie and said friends. He pondered before finally replying, "Can I get some food? I'm starving."

"We can take you somewhere to grab food. Now get your boat locked up and let's get out of here."

Chapter 18

Charlie and the men went peacefully with them. Charlie was not super keen on giving up his weapons, knives, and other fun gadgets he carried on himself. But he could understand why someone would need to do such a thing, especially when they were going to head to what he would assume was a federally run building. There was a new fresh black SUV waiting for them. No one had attempted to set it on fire today. Or at least it didn't appear to have been. But the day was still young, and they did have the guys with them.

Charlie said, "They are expecting me at a certain time. Do your guys understand that? Are they going to be able to meet the times? Are they going to take my boat, or what are the plans?"

"We have everything under control. There's no need to worry. Good thing about being down here is that there's a lot of seized boats. So, there probably won't be a big issue with them realizing the decoy boat isn't too much different. At least that'll be what we are shooting for."

Charlie said, "I need to make a call real quick. I had someone I was supposed to start something for today. You know…before my day went absolutely to hell."

"Well do you remember when we said that we were going to take your phones. That you could have them back after everything is over?"

"Right, but could I use any phone?"

"You mean like a landline?"

"I don't give a shit if it is a cup on a string if I can get this message to let someone know that they need to stay on the down low for a couple days until things with you guys are all done."

"Do you have the number memorized?"

"Fuck…is it really that big of a deal?"

Jim said, "It would seem so. You can call your girlfriend afterwards."

"I'm more worried about the stalker ex-boyfriend that I'm supposed to be looking into. I said I would do something, and I don't want to be the one who doesn't do it and then something happens to her."

Agent Hawk said, "Well, don't worry about it because you don't have a choice in the matter."

"Glad to be here then. I can't wait to get to spend more time with you," Charlie said.

Chapter 19

"When is that prick going to be here?"

"Eduardo, if you ask me something I can't answer one more time, I am going to shoot you and tell Marco that you accidentally fell in the water and a shark ate you. We are far enough out here that he will probably believe me."

Eduardo looked at the water, "I don't see no sharks, Luis."

"You know you could attempt to not make it known that you are the boss's nephew. He must really love your mother."

"Did you want me to tell him that?"

"No, not particularly, Eduardo."

"Then show me a little bit of respect, you see…"

"Eduardo, shut up, there's a boat coming, it looks like Ford's."

"Who else would be out but smugglers and pirates?"

Chapter 20

Agent Hawk hit his radio. He said, "Oyler, stay out of sight, I want you coming in hot with the helicopter as soon as we know they can't start to take off in the boat."

Oyler said, "I have no issues with that. I'd rather let you DEA boys get in there and get shot at. See, we pilots in the DEA are special; there's plenty of you to catch bullets."

"Adorable, just don't fuck around when it's time to come in."

"Holt, do you have that cannon ready to rock?"

Holt said, "I got it, just do your thing. You know I don't mess around when it is time to work, Agent Hawk. Last thing I'm going to do is jeopardize anyone's lives. I got my gunner sitting here and we won't have any issues doing our job. I can promise you that."

"If, by cannon, you mean my highly accurate and lethal long gun then yes, yes I do have it ready."

"You know if you were a guy, I'd whoop your ass."

"You just don't want to look bad having a woman kick the shit out of you, sir."

The two men behind him were laughing before Holt said, "Okay, shut up please. I'm trying to concentrate and a boat moving in the water doesn't make for the best set up. Luckily, I just need to send a round through the engines. Unless they want to swim back home, they won't have many options but to stay put. So long as there isn't a submarine following them. Those cartel guys are pretty damn smart."

"Smart enough to get in trouble, but they haven't gotten caught yet, so they might be doing something right," Agent Hawk said.

Holt whistled and got up. She left her rifle where it was and looked through field glasses, examining everything in the distance. She said, "Jesus Christ, I don't know who they pissed off, but there must have been a helluva arsenal doing it."

She handed over the binoculars, letting Hawk see for himself. He hit his radio saying, "Oyler, get your ass over to that boat and see what in the fuck is going on. I don't know what the fuck happened but fuck me. There's black smoke everywhere."

Oyler didn't answer but she took the helicopter straight over to the coordinates they were supposed to surprise them at. When she got there, Oyler looked to her co-pilot Wilson saying, "Holy shit, what in the fuck happened down there?"

Wilson leaned out looking down. There were still bodies on the boat, but they had been shot to shit and possibly drenched in fuel and lit on fire. It had at one time been a very nice boat but that was no longer. He said, "I don't know, but whoever was doing it was definitely sending a message to who they were pissed off at."

Oyler hit the radio saying, "It is a bust. The men on the boat are all dead, and from what I can see, I don't even know if you'll be able to see who they were. Someone burned the shit out of them."

Hawk hit his phone back to headquarters saying, "Are those guys I brought in earlier still there? They haven't left or spoken to anyone have they?"

"No sir, Agent Hawk. Everyone is still in the room. No one has left and there's no radio signal going in there so no one could have called in the first place to try and tell anyone anything. Is there a problem?"

"Yeah, but there's nothing you can do about it. God damnit, I
wonder what in god's name happened out here?"

Chapter 21

Candace had been checking her phone eagerly. She was curious if Charlie had found out anything. She had tried calling him three times as well. If it hadn't been for Leslie vouching for him and being such a standup guy, she would have been pretty sure that he had completely blown her off. The diner was getting close to closing, so she figured she'd just go about her regular routines and from there maybe she'd just see if she could walk out with Mark and Leslie. Candace kind of hoped that role would be training somewhere and be too busy to be a pain in her ass. When they'd had everything cleaned up for the night, Leslie said, "Candace, why don't you get out of here? Great job today. I hope you shook that rear end enough to get some good tips, if you know what I mean?"

Candace blushed. She preferred giving amazing service over making the men think that they had a shot in hell with her. Of course, she couldn't lie, Charlie had been on her mind today and not just in a professional manner. She couldn't help herself; she didn't hate sleeves of tattoos, muscles, and a guy that didn't try to play any games. She wasn't old but had learned long ago to not waste her time with pieces of shit. Although she'd only had a few dates with Raul, he didn't seem like he'd really ever caught onto that idea, "I haven't counted them yet, but I think I got enough to get pizza and gas tonight."

"Well, I don't want you walking out on your own. Mark, get your sweet ass out from behind the kitchen and go escort our number one…two..no offense, honey, I'm the original. Any who, get her out to her car."

"Anyone messes with us and well they best be fast son of a bitches, because I'm pretty sure we can run like the wind."

Leslie gave him a look, and he put his hands up, already knowing he was defeated. Candace said, "I'm just parked in the alley, Mark. You'll be back to work with her before you know it."

"Oh Joy!"

Chapter 22

A knock came at the door. Fratto turned around seeing Mr. Josh standing there. Fratto nodded and he opened the door. Fratto wasn't sure what to expect but didn't think his bodyguard would need any help. Six of them walked in; they each had a hand on one side of three trunks. Fratto didn't need the money, but he wasn't ever going to look a gift horse in the mouth either. He said, "Did you check the contents already?"

"No offense but yes, I had to sir, I didn't want to worry about there being a bomb in there."

"I'm perfectly alright with that, I appreciate it, actually. The missus hates having the house blown up. Especially with as much time as she puts into it. I don't think that I can afford for her to need to rebuild and furnish one."

Josh knew one thing and that was without any question at all, there was absolutely no way he was making any joke in any manner whatsoever about his wife. He wasn't stupid and wasn't about to see if his boss had a sense of humor about it. There was little question that he probably didn't. Josh motioned for the guys to get out of there. Once they left, he flipped all of the latches on the trunks. Fratto whistled when he saw what looked like an endless sea of hundreds stacked in the containers. He didn't know how much was there but was pretty sure that it was well worth more than his crew had made this month.

Josh said, "Any bonuses for us?"

"Did we lose any guys today?"

"No."

"How about them?"

"Well, we had plenty of things to use to take care of them. By the time they saw us coming, the first rocket was already on its way towards them."

"So, they won't be coming this way anytime soon?"

"Not in living form, Mr. Fratto. Not the two we killed; I can't say as much for their families."

"Good, then I hope their family got the message. If not, we go down there and show them what we think of people coming in on my territory. I will burn their fucking homes to the ground with them and their families in them if they make another push.

Now for the boys I want to send them a little something as a thank you."

"As a thank you for what?"

"I must be in a great mood, Josh."

"Sir?"

"Because if I wanted to explain myself to you, I would shoot myself in the head and become reincarnated so that I could be someone under you. However, this wasn't the case...not at all. If he hadn't asked for that rifle, then I wouldn't have been able to slip a mic in there. We figured out what was going on because of that. So, yeah, I think that works for me."

"I didn't mean to question you...sir."

"Good because if you ever do it again, I'm going to need a new bodyguard."

Josh didn't say anything. He nodded, leaving the cases open, and shut the doors behind him. Fratto smiled, walking to his bed lying down and finishing off a drink that his doc definitely hadn't approved. Lucky for Fratto, it was good to be the boss.

To be continued

By Mike Evans

A quick note from the author, if you enjoyed this book I would very much appreciate you taking a minute to head to Amazon to review this book, or at the least give it a star rating, please. Clicking this will take you to review.

Please see below for additional info by Mike Evans
Mike's newsletter don't miss out on any news!
http://www.tinyurl.com/evansnews

Mike Evans Facebook Author Page
https://www.facebook.com/MikeEvansAuthor

Contact Email
m.evansauthor@gmail.com

Mike Evans on Amazon
https://www.amazon.com/Mike-Evans/e/B00IQ9Z75A

Do you love an action book?

Charlie Ford Adventure Series

Gabriel Series

Buried: Broken oaths

The Operator

Want zombies?

Vacation from Hell Series

Zombies on The Block Series

The Orphans Series

Zombies and Chainsaws Series

Looking for some true-crime style serial killer fiction?

The Uninvited Series

Voices in My Head

Are the devil, demons, and holy wars your thing?

Demons Beware Series

Deal with The Devil

9 798838 640529